Julian Sharman

A Cursory History of Swearing

Julian Sharman

A Cursory History of Swearing

ISBN/EAN: 9783337338152

Printed in Europe, USA, Canada, Australia, Japan

Cover: Foto ©Andreas Hilbeck / pixelio.de

More available books at **www.hansebooks.com**

CURSORY

.

HISTORY OF SWEARING.

BY

JULIAN SHARMAN.

"Ha! this fellow is worse than me; what, does he swear with pen and ink?"—*The Tatler*, No. 13.

LONDON:

J. C. NIMMO AND BAIN,
14, KING WILLIAM STREET, STRAND, W.C.
1884.

CONTENTS.

CHAPTER I.

CHAPTER II.

CHAPTER III.

CHAPTER IV.

CHAPTER V.

CHAPTER VI.

CHAPTER VII.

CHAPTER VIII.

CHAPTER IX.

A

CURSORY

HISTORY OF SWEARING.

CHAPTER I.

AT THE SCUFFLERS' CLUB.

"'Our armies swore terribly in Flanders,' said my uncle
Toby, 'but nothing to this.'"—*Tristram Shandy*.

IT lay in the heart of Bohemia. It was approached
through a labyrinth of streets that grew denser and
darker as one neared the precincts of the club. Could
any of the brother Scufflers have seen the neighbourhood
by day, it would have presented an appearance dismal
and sordid enough. Dealers in faded wardrobes,—
merchants in tinsel and *rouge de théâtre*,—retailers of
wigs and fleshings and all manner of stage wares,
seemed one with another to have made the locality
their home. One missed certainly the bone-sellers and
refuse-sifters of the adjacent Clare Market, and one was

spared the cheap cosmetic shops and smug undertakers
of the neighbouring Soho. But you were recompensed,
here in the heart of mid-Bohemia, by the all-pervading
odour of potations and provisions,—of banquets long
past, and of banquets that were yet to come.

What wonderful odours are those that emanate from
this quarter of the town! The dank vapours of Covent
Garden are sweet in the nostrils of many a cockney
reveller. There is no orange-peel so perfumed as the
Drury orange-peel that has been concentrating its
fragrance round the boards of Thespis since the days
when Mohun and Hart, and Shatterel and Betterton
strutted on the bare planks of the Cockpit. No scent
of printer's ink is more refreshing than that which
adheres to the yards of flimsy playbill still hawked
about by itinerant vendors. But the whole place has
through the day-time a blear-eyed, a drunk-over-night
appearance. It is like a man who is never at his best
until he has supped or dined. From morn till twilight
it wears this sullen and uncared-for look. Wait until
nightfall, and it will positively glisten with lamps and
gleam with merriment. No wonder, therefore, that it
has been the birthplace of so many of those midnight
carousing dens, into one of which we are tremulously
seeking to enter.

It was what is called a literary and theatrical club, the Scufflers. It was literary in so far that the majority of its members lay down at night with unrealised dreams of authorship. It was theatrical to the extent that many a one was the possessor of an unacted drama coiled up in his breast coat-pocket, and was to be seen surging about managers' doors, only waiting the glance of favour to fall upon author and manuscript. Nor was this literary impulsion entirely without fruit-bearing. Scufflers had been known to rush breathlessly into the club-room at the approach of midnight, and in an excited and panting condition have been heard to sing out for pens and paper, as the morning press would wait for no man. Personally the accomplishments of the members were many and varied. The great *primus* and leader of the club was a man who was alleged to dash off a leading article, take a hand at whist, and tackle a dish of kidneys at one and the same time.

We must now be supposed to have reached the entrance of the hostelry, for indeed it was a Covent Garden tavern and nothing more.

We commence to grope our way along the moulder-ing, unlit passage that gives access to the one apartment tenanted by the club, in which their cheerful delibera-

tions are now proceeding. Time cannot efface t
memory of that green-baize door at the end of tl
passage, where we were very properly brought to
stand on that first evening of our initiation. Nev
shall we forget how momentous seemed the issues tl
were depending in that inner chamber, as the announc
ment that there was a "stranger at the gates" w
evidently being briskly canvassed there. To have t
unquestioned privilege of passing and repassing th
mystic portal, the barrier as it seemed between all t
rhapsody and the syntax of this weary world, promise
to be one of those pleasures that would well-nigh
imperishable.

The apartment entered, it was easy to discern tl
manner of men who had placed their mark upon i
walls and wainscots. There was no lack of artist for
in many of the daubs that were let into the panellin
to remain rugged monuments of the skill of tl
frequenters of that chamber. A piano there was th
had seen better days, and was yet to see considerabl
worse ones, if in our recollection of the ultimate dispers
of the property of the club we are not mistaken. The
there were the pipe-racks. Anything more eloquer
can scarcely be imagined than the story unfolded b
these mute implements of smoking. Every pip

ssessed its decided characteristic and was distinctly
fferent from its neighbour. Some showed themselves
 conceited pipes ; some were light and sparkish, others
nderous and clumsy. Leave yourself alone with these
icks of briar or cherry-wood and you could readily
ve brought to mind their absent owners,—the man
ho sang a good song, the youngster given to practical
kes, the patriarch, strong in argument, invincible in
bate,—in fact you could easily have helped yourself to
 inventory of the members of the club. The rest of
le furniture of the room consisted of a large oblong table,
rrounded by chairs of various patterns, the former of
hich on the night we first beheld it literally groaned
ith the weight of "rabbits" and foaming tankards.
tay ; food for the mind was not neglected, as how should
be ? in that assembly-room. By virtue of the care of
pile of fly-blown magazines, and as far as we can re-
ember of a few odd volumes of ' Ruff's Guide ' and a
White's Farriery,' we became in course of time the
ected librarian of the Scufflers' Club.

Although not a flourishing community in the matter
' finances, there were instances in plenty of great
ndness and liberality displayed by Scuffler unto
uffler. There ‿were times when they brought out
eir myrrh and cassia, their spikenard and oil of price.

B

When, one bitter winter morning, an unhappy Scuffler came shivering out of the debtors' side of the City Prison, they did not beat about the bush and hesitate at receiving him. Neither did they stand on any dignity or whisper any threat of expulsion. They did nothing of this kind, they simply made him drunk. It is, we hope, quite clear that these gentlemen were not professors of any sort of austerity.

It may have already dawned upon the reader that there can hardly have existed a fraternity boasting any such name as the one we have allotted to it. In this much the reader is perfectly right. The club had a title strikingly similar to that which we have adopted, and the thin disguise has only been suggested from a circumstance that we may at once frankly disclose. Suspended over the club chimney-piece was the usual notice-board, a perfect encyclopædia in its way, and covered with a trellis-work of crimson tape for the purpose of retaining the various *affiches*. In this way were displayed, from day to day, the cards and letters intended for the members of the club. For so long a time did they frequently remain exhibited, and so complete a disregard did the owners manifest for their property, that the appearance of each packet often grew quite familiar to the frequenters of the place. The individuality of the writer might be often guessed from the evidence of the various superscriptions, and when all other sources of amusement failed the contents of this stationary post-office formed a fair staple of banter and merry comment. There were to be seen perfumed and coronetted envelopes addressed to quasi-fashionable members. These were gentlemen who never seemed to call and claim their belongings. Then there were letters reputed to emanate from the great publishing houses, and there were missives surmounted with well-known theatrical monograms that were alleged to forward brilliant offers of engagements. In fact it was by the aid of such simple nest-eggs as these that the men managed to establish reputations. But there was one class of correspondence that obviously was not intended for much publicity. These were the letters couched in feminine handwriting, none of the neatest, whose tremulous writers, in addressing their envelopes, rarely succeeded in hitting off the proper style and title of the club. The early looker-in might have made a useful study of these shaky epistles,—scrawls painfully executed by milliners and toy-women. It was on the cover of one of such effusions, even worse written and worse spelt than they usually were, that we first saw the inscription, the " Scufflers' Club."

Although some years have passed since first we were made free of that circle, distinctly do we remember the manner of our greeting—" This," said our introducer, " is a room rendered famous by the celebrated Addison." He emphasised the "celebrated" owing to an evident misgiving that we might not perhaps be intimate with the name of that personage. " Kitty Clive, the actress," he continued, "lodged in the upper floors,"—which was true—"and Dr. Johnson is said to have worn away the wainscot with his wig in the further corner,"—which was not. We were already lingering over the notice-board and letter-rack, reminded probably by the associations of a similar contrivance at Will's Coffee House, when Parson Swift came in the mornings to seek for letters from Stella, when the voice of our cicerone again summoned us. " Drop into a seat," it whispered, " and I'll show you the best men in London."

The best men in London were engaged for the most part in imbibing various amber-coloured fluids, and shouting out at intervals the burden of a well-known chorus. An entertainment known as a " sing-song " was vociferously going on. Vocalisation of a very fair order was being given, whenever any one of the hearty Scufflers had sufficiently wetted his throat to " oblige." We were in time to hear the ' Friar of Orders Gray ' performed very creditably, and 'When Joan's ale was new' brought out a ringing chorus. We must have stayed some hours in listening to this minstrelsy. Hospital songs, ditties well-known at Bartholomew's and Guy's; poaching songs that bore the flavour of the honest shire of Somerset; pieces from the comic operas; all were given with the utmost good-humour and vivacity. But what seemed most to invigorate the spirits of the Scufflers was a song that had been demanded more than once during the evening and was at length only given after extreme pressure upon the part of the audience. We do not know the name of the song; we are not certain we should recollect the tune; but we are positive of the words, such of them at least as formed the refrain of the melody. In every stanza there was held up to reprobation some unpopular type. The severer virtues were no less mercilessly handled, while all authority of the more invidious kind, from that of the beak to that of the exciseman, was subjected to the same unceremonious treatment. Every versicle—well do we remember it—concluded with the exordium, "Damn their eyes!" Never can we forget the rapturous reception that was accorded to this piece of harmony. The men literally shrieked with delight. "Damn their eyes!"—they grasped convulsively at

tumblers and decanters and banged them on the table.
"Damn their eyes!"—they hurrahed, they shouted,
they raved, they swore. "Damn their eyes!"—they
bestrode chairs and benches, as they might have
bestridden hobby-horses, and tournamented about the
room. Was this then the pæan or war-song of the
Scufflers' Club?

As with the morning light we came to reflect upon
the midnight orgie, we felt we had opened a chapter in
a strange history, and that history a history of swearing.

We can hardly bring our pen to write the very title
of this book without being reminded of an incident
that has amused while it has displeased us. It is now
very many years ago that a kind relative brought the
present writer, then a child at a dame's school, a handsome copy of the ' Vicar of Wakefield,' and thenceforward
for a time that bitter schoolhouse bade fair to be made
bright and joyous with the doings of the simple men
and women whose story the gentle Goldsmith has
recorded. What possible objection could be uttered
against so innocent a tale? None the less however did
our worthy preceptress take occasion to remonstrate.
"Does not that book concern females?" asked she.
Our friend could have had no reply prepared that was
fitted to so insidious a reproach. "Ah! well," was the

quiet rejoinder, "but poor Goldsmith did not mean badly."

If such, then, be the measure dealt out to the more disciplined champions in the strife with human error, what sort of accord will be given to the present unharnessed and ill-caparisoned writer, who attempts, let it be hoped not ill-naturedly, to cope with one of the more rosy-faced forms of sinfulness. That he will be assailed from the higher latitudes of prudery he has a right to expect. That the very novelty of the venture will pass as an affront to some portion of his readers there is only reason to anticipate. That even the more indulgent will cast looks of suspicion upon his pirate ensign is a circumstance he can conceal as little as he can regret it.

As the matter stands, a poor devil of an author is proposing an expedition into regions that, despite many hundred years of literary enterprise, are still remote and untravelled. It were not surprising therefore at the outset that his readers should inquire if he is sincere and reliable, or whether on the contrary he is counterfeiting honesty with a sanctimonious face. It were perhaps right they should be assured that the trip is really intended for their welfare, and that the skipper is not given to risk the safety of his craft for a mere capful

of wind.   But conceding that it is natural to raise these
doubts at the threshold of the journey, the author has it
in his power to give little or no assurance of the sincerity
of his undertaking.   Whatever notion he may entertain
of his own, or of other people's morality, he has no
opinion whatever of their professions of it.   He refrains
therefore from giving any warranty of the soundness of
his wares.

Save but for this.   He has often been vexed, and
puzzled as well as vexed, at one great discord that has
been sent upon the world.   Yielding and kindly as it
may have been to them, men have not scrupled to cast
defiance and calumny upon this forbearing earth and to
hurl hissing curses at its abundance and its pervading
spirit of forgiveness.   Not since the labour of men's
hands began have they ceased to furrow it with menace
and sow it with imprecation, cursing while their
very corn ripens under midsummer skies, cursing as
they gather in their store of wine and victual.   What
does it mean?   What *can* it mean?   Whence has it
arisen, and whither does it tend?   These are among
the questions that have influenced the mind of the
writer in considering the purview of his book.

The misfortune that is often experienced in handling
any subject lying wide of the beaten track does not

necessarily arise from the inherent viciousness of the
subject itself, but from the fact that a large number of
people have previously arrived at painful impressions
concerning it. It is therefore an obligation cast upon
a writer to treat these preconceived notions with the
utmost tenderness and respect. Personally one may
hold the art of swearing in perfect indifference, being
neither among the number of swearers oneself nor
having any very strong feeling of reprobation towards
its more active adherents. But despite a certain in-
clination that we feel to apologise for what we hold to
be the silliest of vices, we are forced to recollect that to
many the offence will always appear in anything but a
trivial light. It is therefore obligatory upon us to
abstain as far as possible from referring to expressions
that are calculated to alarm. At the close of the last
century there existed a religious sect who were in
favour of abandoning the use of clothing. Blake, the
poet, was one of these enthusiasts, and his wife also.
The holders of this convenient doctrine were in the
habit of presenting themselves in their households as
naked as they were born. In so acting we may be
sure they were only in keeping with their sober
convictions, and that they were ready to maintain in
argument the thorough soundness and consistency of

their views. For aught we know to the contrary, this naked doctrine may of itself have been right, but the misfortune which continued, and for the matter of that still continues, to be felt, was that by far the larger portion of humanity retained a decided prejudice in favour of apparel. So long as the disciple of the Adamite school was contented to denude himself in his own particular circle there may have been no positive harm, but it would scarcely have been open to a member of that fraternity to have walked down Fleet Street like an ancient Briton. The thinker also who takes upon himself to theorise in a manner apart from any considerable section of humanity, is no less bound to entertain a fitting respect for the notions, even to the mistaken notions, with which that section is animated. Whatever his own disposition towards an absolute freedom of expression, he is under the obligation of attiring his ideas in the manner habituated to the tastes of his listeners.

Happily, however, there is possible a middle course. We need not grovel in the sinks and cellars, neither need we ruminate upon the house-tops. We can settle ourselves as it were, in that easy, neutral smoking-room of literature, where we can put off broadcloth for fustian ; and utter our heresies with still a chance left us of being forgiven. Here we may expect to meet only with that mature and seasoned criticism that holds the scale very evenly between the outspoken and the insolent. While by no means to be accounted friendly towards the vile excrescences of swearing, the ordinary man of the world is not to be repelled by every street oath, or put to lasting confusion by every passing word of unseemliness. To put it upon no higher ground than that of mere custom, it were too arrogant to assume abhorrence of a practice that is as trite and customary as the incidents of one's daily rounds. Besides, there is another explanation for the supineness that is exhibited towards errors of this description. It could be shown how, by a slight mental process, the extravagances and the follies of other men are capable of offering a subtle compliment to a person's understanding. They set it off. They adorn what he fancies to be his intellectual superiority, and he is not indisposed in consequence to extend a feeble patronage towards the very vices which, did he not experience ever so slight a benefit from them, he would otherwise be foremost in decrying. Again, it were too obviously inconsistent to take our repose in a tavern and yet direct our homilies at tavern habits, at the enormity of tobacco-smoking or of drinking drams.

And yet it may be possible for most of us to go back to no distant time when we sickened at the scent of the finest Virginian and the juice of the juniper was bitter. It was not a great while ago certainly!

A great while ago! Say, courteous and gentle— nay, uncourteous and ungentle reader—can you so far travel back in your recollection as to recall your first parting from all that was homely and kindly and familiar? Do you remember the first separation from the half-score of faces that to you had peopled the earth and represented the whole sum and mystery of living? Can you now realise that desolate night, closing in upon the blank, colourless day, the lonely stages, the harsh grating of the wheels, all the impressions in fact of that long, pitiful journey that once came as a barrier between you and childish innocence? And then the arrival at that strange school; how hollow the laughter of the men, how shrill the chirp and twitter of the women! Do you remember the comfortless morrow that brought the first contact with your boy associates? They were probably harmless and good-natured enough, those uncouth, ill-fashioned boys, and doubtless there were among them many who would have been quick to requite a wrong and eager to soothe any injury. But how they pained you with

their jests; how they bruised you in their boisterous
play; how old they looked to your young eyes; how
full of wiles and intrigue and savagery! And then
their talk! not the mild caressing talk of the lips you
loved, of the forms you knew, but loud and brazen, and
savouring of cunning and high-handedness. And in
their quarrels and their games, they swore—those boys
swore; not all of them be it hoped, but the great
giants and paladins among them who seemed to bear
rule and mastery with whips and thongs. Many a
time before, perhaps, you may have been seized with
faintness and aversion at some imagined evil, that
might as well have been enacted in some distant
planet. But now the horror was no longer slumbering
or remote; it was awake and crying at your door.
Now, and within a few hours, were disclosed the
sources of all the aimless brutalities, all the self-
asserting iniquities that have played such havoc in an
erring world. And, as these knowing fellows chattered
over their scraps of worldly wisdom, and as their puny
curses were bandied round, it seemed as if some great
treason were being poured out, a trespass alike against
God in heaven and the folks at home.

How could one know at that young age that all one
heard was not really villainous, that much of it indeed

was mere *brusquerie*, rough-ridden perhaps, but brisk
and spirited? How should one understand that the
tones which seemed so harsh and jarring belonged in
truth to a very code of sprightliness? But a few
weeks more perhaps, and you too had taken the ring of
this brazen metal. You had perceived upon what
measure of aggression, upon what rasping unkindnesses,
the applause of your fellows was bestowed. To violate
every rule with fearless indifference, to be abreast with
every move that was daring or was dexterous, these
were the feats by which approval was won. In the
matter of swearing you might have remained only an
unwilling dabbler, only a mixer and meddler in the
luxury, were it not that occasion came when you were
solemnly arraigned for the offence, and straightway
branded as a culprit. It is in this way that offences
come. So you may have received your punishment
and have revolted under it; and perhaps you may have
had a right to revolt. For our spiritual pastors, in
judging of our virtues, too often endowed us with the
capacities of children, and in judging of our vices they
endowed us with the capacities of men.

In that our early play-time, of which we have been
speaking, we distinctly call to mind two errant school-
fellows, brought together by kindred tastes, though

differing in temper and disposition. Each is of an age when the world resembles only some May-day morning, and at the moment we are recalling them they have no other occupation than that of dreamily rambling through the fields and lanes, delighted with the breezy country-side, and luxuriating in their own boyish out-pourings. They had conceived this mutual liking because each felt the other to be in true sympathy with nature, and to be capable of discerning the wonderful enchantments of poetry and cadence. They had found a warm and unselfish delight in ministering to the other's appreciation. They could drink in great draughts of beauty from the chalice so unsparingly held out by Shelley or Goethe, by Wordsworth or Byron. They could revel in the rugged measures of 'Marmion,' in the whirl and clatter of the 'Last Minstrel.' They could be gay with the loves of the Two Gentlemen, or kindle at the woes of Imogen or the sorrows of Effie Deans.

And so, in such senseless manner, they are now skirting the golden harvest-fields, recalling perhaps the bright fancy that has given the 'Skylark' to the world, or mindful of "liquid Peneus" and "darkened Tempe." Presently there burst out of the thicket two ruffians, with rags torn and bespattered, caked with summer's dust and mildewed by winter's rain. As they approached their voices sounded devilish and unearthly. They raised one long plaint of deep-toned, hard-set blasphemy. Their every word was shotted with an oath. Hoarse with brandy, bitter with malevolence, they cursed at the plenty of the harvest,—at the patient cattle grazing in the fields,—at the crimson poppy blowing in the ditch,—at the buzzing insects, at the ripening orchards. They cursed at the luck of the skittle-alley; they cursed at the insolence of the rulers of the land. When the devil made war with heaven, this must have been the roar of his artillery.

We looked at our friend—for this has become a personal narrative, as may already have been conjectured—and we marked the pain and sorrow of heart that had visibly overcome him. Silently he seemed to implore protection from the great span of universe surrounding us—for it was he who was the gentler and more loyal spirit of the two. Then, as the curses and ribaldry died away, he emerged slowly as from beneath a stupefying load. Presently he fell to talking of the strange perverseness with which men have always clung to this undying evil, and cited the Levitical story of "the son of the Israelitish woman,"—the impious oaths demanded of old time by emperors and satraps, and the resistance of the martyred Polycarp.

Who knows but that at that moment we may have thought our friend little better than a fool, and his words the drivel of idiotcy? We have said somewhere, speaking of morality, that we have no opinion of professions of it. It must be known that he was mild and retiring and submissive. He could not give blow for blow as other boys could; he could not cheat or lie or gamble as other boys did. He was more awkward of limb and coarser dressed. Anyhow, we have set down here some of our first impressions of swearing, and now we are cursorily writing its history.

CHAPTER II.

" Now don't let us give ourselves a parcel of airs and pretend
that the oaths we make free with in this land of liberty of ours
are our own ; and because we have the spirit to swear them,—
imagine that we have had the wit to invent them too."— *Tristram
Shundy.*

WHEN Hesiod fabled the god of oaths to be the son
of Discord, the poet could hardly have foreseen the
grim reality that would attach to his satiric allegory.
It is now a very small thing—a matter of no consequence at all—that serious and well-meaning men once
attested their assertions by making passing reference
to Minerva or Helios. But yet is it none the less
necessary to realise that they made such reference
for the express purpose of being believed, and that
when not pronouncing one or other of these forms of
speech, they ran a strong chance of being absolutely
disbelieved.

Hesiod has dimly chronicled the genealogy of
oaths. But it was for other generations to chronicle
their posterity, to hear them derided in the amphi-
theatre, and to see the divinities that inspired them

shattered and broken down. But there is a singular survival and continuity of the ancient practice: men still swear by Jove.

A like process of declension seems to have gone on in all countries and in the same fashion. To begin with, the origin of all swearing was the same—the one intense dread of falsehood against which as yet no laws were sufficient to guard. Fancy the mortal distress of barbarian man when he first wakes to the belief that his enemies can, by smooth speech, wrest from his hands what his prowess or his labour has acquired. No art that he is aware of can pervert the action of tongues set falsely going. Seeing how illimitable is the crop of words, he may even imagine a plague of lies that will fall thick about him like locusts or caterpillars; and then arrives the old expedient. Men fasten upon a symbol such, as it is hoped, the hardiest will revere, and syllable it out as evidence of truth.

If we are not mistaken, it may even be said that the degree of refinement that a community has attained is discernible by taking as a standpoint the merchantable character of truth. Wherever civilisation is advancing, the ultimate unserviceability of lying becomes the more apparent, and there ensues in consequence a depreciation in the value of veracity. The more widely truth is

recognised, the more does it deteriorate in price, while
falsehood ceases to arouse its former measure of reprobation.   Then it is, and not, indeed, until then, that the old
blundering remedy by means of oaths and oath-taking
is laid aside as out of date and no longer availing.
Nowadays, at least among most races of mankind, the
ordinary inducements to veracity are of themselves felt
to be sufficiently powerful as to leave no ground for
contending that truthfulness should be the subject of
rewards and bounties.   No money value is attached as
of right to the performance of an obvious duty, but in
remoter times the recognition of such a doctrine, could
it have been recognised at all, would have spared the
coffers of Roman sesterces and have made the work of
the Athenian pay-clerks hang lightly on their hands.
The fact would seem to be that the prevalency of this
deliberative swearing will always be found in inverse
ratio to the prevalency of truth.

The later civilisations may, therefore, be said to have
profited by centuries of untruthfulness in that they have
learnt the preponderating advantages of an intelligible
code of truth.   To seek an illustration by comparison of
two periods perfectly dissimilar, it may be affirmed that
there was no greater proportion of really truthful men
in France at the period, say, of Voltaire, than twelve

hundred years previously at the period of Gregory of Tours. But the countrymen of Voltaire had become fairly apprised of the expediency of common veracity, and their assertions, in consequence, were not accustomed to be disbelieved. But among the Frédégondes, the Clotaires, and the Cunégondes of Gregory's Frankish history, the case is wholly different. In that day it might almost be supposed from a perusal of the work that the faculty of truth-telling was lost, or more correctly that it had never arisen, so necessary was it considered to put a statement to the severest test before the possibility of its accuracy could be admitted. In an indulgent, selfish, but disciplined civilisation, a statement is generally presumed to be true which bears the ordinary impress of veracity. In periods considerably less intellectual and enlightened, we shall find that nothing is presumed to be true until it has been subjected to a searching process of corroboration. It is in fact this process of corroboration that has furnished all ranks of swearers with their necessary side-arms and equipment.

In the two conditions of society we have just indicated, there is revealed at once the cause and effect of promiscuous oath-taking. The one, incredulous and diffident of belief, imposes oath upon oath as its natural

safeguard, and engages in an unremitting struggle to
render the bond of truthfulness subservient to a
despotic will.   The other is weary of forms that have
outlived whatever spirit was once imparted them; it
has snapped asunder the galling fetters, and made
sportive capital of the lumber that remains.   An inter-
vening age of irony probably sufficed to undermine the
sanctity of the swearing obligation, until at last the
oath of more sober times has come to be a common
catchword, or the fustian ornament of somewhat spirited
talk.   In short, we shall always find that the sonorous
expletive of recent days is nothing else than the once
deliberative oath of Christian piety.

Human ingenuity has seldom been more industri-
ously employed than in attempting to restore successive
breaches in the observances of swearing.   Among the
Western nations, it is said, religious sentiment had
nothing to do with the foundation of the usage.   With
them swearing is represented to have been of purely
military origin, and the oaths taken upon sword and
javelin to have owed nothing to the emotions of piety.
The process undergone by the military oath of Gaul
before it finally culminated in an expression of religious
import, was of a very slow and gradual kind.   The
Franks were accustomed to appeal to the drawn sword

as being the only arbiter of existence. In course of time the sanctity of this engagement was broken through, and to ensure due regard for the solemnity of the oath, it was found necessary to make the weapon the subject of an impressive ceremony. By the capitularies of Dagobert, the sword and harness of the warrior were required to be consecrated. Still later, the name of God was brought into the compact. "If two neighbours," ordains King Dagobert, "are in dispute as to the boundary of their possessions, let them bring into the camp a turf of the disputed territory; and each, with hands resting on the points of their swords, and taking God to be the witness of the truth, shall give battle until victory decides the question." Not only was the military oath superseded; but, as years wore on, even these additional guarantees proved themselves to be ineffectual. The interposition of saints next came to be deemed essential, and again with the most conflicting results. When Chilperic and his brothers divided the kingdom of Clotaire, and swore never to enter the capital except as allies, their treaty was ratified by oaths taken in the name of Saint Hilaire, Saint Policeute, and Saint Martin. As time advanced, these further methods of precaution in their turn proved abortive. Chilperic, seizing Paris in contravention of

his oath, carried as an antidote the relics of more potent
and illustrious saints in the van of his victorious army.
So dangerous a precedent being once admitted, it
became necessary to resort to still other expedients.
It was thought as well to ascertain with what degree of
veaeration the intending swearer might happen to
regard that particular member of the calendar whose
name was proposed to be invoked. In doubtful cases,
therefore, it was not unusual to conduct a deponent
from one shrine to another, that among the multitude
of oaths one of them at least might prove effectual.
A son of Clotaire, being plied by a rebel agent with
insurrectionary advice, thought it prudent to conduct
his adviser before the altars of no less than twelve
churches before he felt himself justified in listening to
the representations that were offered him.

It would seem, indeed, from the practice of half
barbarous nations, that so far from the Deity, or even
the monuments of religion, being the immediate subject
of the swearing obligation, these were practically the
most remote. During the second siege of Rome by the
Goths, the ministers of Honorius were called upon to
swear solemnly that they would refuse to entertain any
overtures of peace, and would wage implacable warfare
upon the enemy. With great difficulty were they

induced to confirm this engagement with an oath taken by the head of the emperor. This formula was the most impressive and, in effect, the most binding that could well have been resorted to, and it is reported by Gibbon that the ministers were heard to declare that had the same oath been taken by the name of the Deity they would have held themselves free to depart from it. In doing blind obeisance to the arms of warfare or the symbols of authority, the ancient world only varied from the modern as the usages of religion differ from those of idolatry. In Rome, we are told, the spear was sacred to Juno, and in the province of Rhegium was worshipped as Mars. In Scythia the sword was glorified as the messenger of life and death. And it is to be noticed as an evidence of the superstitious sanctity that pervaded warlike implements, that in Rome, according to a half-religious rite, the hair of newly-married women was parted with the point of a spear. The oaths, in fine, of the Western military nations distinctly breathe of the spirit of war, while those of the more dreamful Eastern world are redolent of light and air, of sun and shade. To this day in Servia the popular forms of swearing express dependence and reliance upon the powers of nature. *Taku mi Suntza*, So help' me sun; *Taku mi Semlje*,

So help me earth, are the methods of asseveration that are in every-day use.

That period in modern history at which the deliberative oath had assumed something of its ultimate shape is marked by the occurrence of one singular invasion of its solemnity. The incident we refer to is the charge preferred by Thomas-à-Becket against John the Marshal, to the effect that he had sworn upon a "book of old songs" instead of upon the sacred writings which had then become the proper instruments for this purpose. Indeed, in tracing the history of these observances it would seem as if an endeavour was being constantly made to frustrate the aims and ends of swearing, and that the more Christian modes were only resorted to when every pagan method had been found inoperative. To swear upon the authority of everything that was terrible or grotesque—by the sword or javelin of a conquering nation, as by the love-token on a maiden's sleeve; * by the sepulchre of a debtor; † by the abbey church at Glastonbury, ‡ or by the price of the potter's field §— these were expedients that had been tried and been forsaken before the modern forms of swearing were reached. Like the time-expired worship of the divinities

---

* Ducange.   † The laws of Hoel the Good.
‡ Chronicle of Robert of Gloucester.   § Ducange.

of the mythology that, in the one solitary temple of
Mount Casano, was maintained for some hundred years
after the gods of Olympus had been deposed: so the
impious oaths of pagandom continued to jostle and
wrestle with those of Christianity for many centuries
after authority had pronounced their doom. "Olympian
Jupiter!" exclaims Aristophanes, at the mention of that
oath, "to think of your believing in Jupiter, as old as
you are!"

How stubbornly the ground was contested may be
inferred from the enactments of civil and ecclesias-
tical law. So early as the ninth century, Justinian
prescribed the punishment of death for the offence of
swearing by the limbs of God. The code that prevailed
in the northern districts of Britain was more severe than
any that was enforced elsewhere in these islands. By
statutes of Donald VI. and Kenneth II., the penalty of
cutting out the tongue was inflicted upon swearers. In
France, Charlemagne legislated expressly against the
practice of impious oath-taking, and by an edict of
Philip II. swearers were condemned to drowning in
the Seine.* The Council of Constantinople passed a
sentence of excommunication upon the swearers of
heathen oaths.

* Mezeray, ii. 121.

To how great an extent this unmeaning discord disturbed the current of mediæval life may be seen from an examination of contemporary literature. In particular, we may instance an early fragment that has come down to us, and was evidently intended as a glowing satire upon the prevalence of the abuse. It is called the 'Moralité des Blasphémateurs,' and was issued from the Paris press in the early part of the sixteenth century. The whole design of the piece is to exhibit the supposed agency of the potentates of Hell in proselytising mankind towards the adoption of the most abhorrent blasphemy. Satan, according to demonologists once the governor of the north of Heaven, is now a feudatory prince in the kingdom of Beelzebub. He is presumed to act under the orders of Lucifer, the judge of Hell, and is joined in his commission by Behemoth, the henchman and cupbearer of the infernal chiefs. There is a sufficiency of invective in the opening greeting of these personages that was doubtless calculated to add to the repulsive character of the performance:—

> "Sathan, ennemy traistre et faulx,
> Où es tu mauldict loricart?"

To which Satan replies:—

> "Que veulx tu, mauldict Lucifer?
> Que te fault-il, beste saulvaige?"

Their salutation finished, these worthies proceed to recount the sport they have had on earth. Satan has visited the land of France, where he has spent his time in the company of horse-stealers and cattle-lifters, fellows, he assures them, who have no thought for mass or vespers; and he has left them feasting day and night, getting as drunk as herons. This account of his stewardship seems to give but small satisfaction to Lucifer, who thereupon bids his followers—

> " Allez tost par mons et par vaulx
> Faire jurer le nom de Dieu
> A garses et à garsonneaulx
> En toute place et en tout lieu.
> C'est une belle operation
> De jurer Dieu à chascun point."

This strain of conversation continues through over a hundred pages of closely-printed matter, and is only varied by the exordiums of certain more admirable characters, who are introduced, as we must suppose, to point a moral to the story.

The state of feeling disclosed by this offensive farce shows plainly, even at that time, that the public which tolerated it had passed out of a state of mere supineness and had assumed an attitude of disrespect and defiance towards the authority of oaths. The system had been

allowed to overreach itself, and thenceforward its set
forms and all the paraphernalia that pertained to them
were made over to the service of criminality and to the
uses of violent speech. The modern practice of swearing, in either its flippant or vituperative shape, is
derived from the break-up of the process once devised as
a protection of truthfulness and fair dealing. So nearly
allied have been the oaths of piety and statecraft with
those of violence and malice, that the severer thinkers,
whether Lollards, Puritans, or Quakers, have waged a
war of extermination against both alike. They have
contended, and with some amount of probability, that
these jarring expletives of passion and irreligion have
only been perpetuated by reason of the familiarity that
has ensued from the undue exaction of legal tests.
The same stubbornness with which they combated the
evil in endless tracts and broadsides they maintained
before courts and inquisitions. At the Lancaster
Assizes of 1664, George Fox and Mrs. Margaret Fell
stood upon their trial for refusing to conform. " I have
never laid my hand on the book to swear in all my
life," urged the woman. "I do not care if I never hear
an oath read, for the land mourns because of oaths."
And then appealing to the jury she exclaims: " I was
bred and born in this county and never have been at

this assize before. I am a widow, and my estate is a dowry, and I have five children unpreferred."

There was one device of oath-taking, half pagan and half barbaric, which but very slowly relaxed its hold on Christian Europe. We have spoken of the oath upon the sword—the oath of ancient Scythia, the oath of the Antigone of Euripedes. In the terrors of an isolated death, remote from all the outward appliances of his faith, the stricken warrior found consolation in raising before his vision the hilt of his scabbardless sword. The tapering metal-hafted blade threw the shadow of a cross upon the dying soldier, and to this rude emblem the poor fevered lips would stammer out their last words of petition. The sword had become a revered symbol conveying to the departing the hope of divine favour and intercession. This thought so powerfully arrested the imagination that it did not relinquish its grasp when a period of security had succeeded a reign of bloodshed and danger. In the traditions of Denmark, the oath upon the sword-hilt was preserved in a sp'rit of deep solemnity. Later, in English history, the King-Maker took his vows upon the cross of his bared steel, and the custom lingered in effigy to the days of Elizabeth, when the fencing-masters, practising their calling at the Bear Garden, were required to take an

oath upon their rapier's hilt to carry themselves
honourably in their profession.* The gravity with
which this form of conjuration is approached by
Hamlet's followers is evident from the passage:—

> " *Hor.* } My lord, we will not.
> *Mar.*
>
> *Hamlet.* Nay, but swear it.
>
> *Hor.* In faith, my lord, not I.
>
> *Ghost* (beneath). Swear!
>
> *Hamlet.* Ha, ha, boy! say'st thou so? art there, true-
> penny?
> Come on—you hear this fellow in the cellarage,
> Consent to swear.
>
> *Hor.* Propose the oath, my lord.
>
> *Hamlet.* Never to speak of this that you have seen, ·
> Swear by my sword."

The ground that we have thus far traversed is really
one of a remarkable struggle, that has not abated even
in our time. It is not the intention of this essay to
follow the history of judicial oath-taking, or of the
attestations that would seem to be demanded by con-

---

* Sloane MS. No. 2530, xxvi. D.; a manuscript giving details of the
grades of students and masters of fence, and of the ceremonial attending
taking their degrees. The oath runs, " First you shall swear, so help
you God and halidome, and by all the christendome which God gave you
at the fount stone, and by the cross of this sword which doth represent
unto you the cross which our Saviour suffered his most painful deathe
upon," &c.

science or religion. But it must be remembered that the subject of vituperative swearing is so interwoven with that of these legal and religious ordinances, that the consideration of them must be frequently forced upon us. But whilst doing so it should be no less borne in mind that we are never really losing sight of the object we have in view. We aim simply at disinterring a neglected, possibly a justly neglected, chapter in the world's social history, and are called upon to judge both of the tree and its fruit, of the seed and the grain.

CHAPTER III.

THE BRITISH SHIBBOLETH.

"Pantagruel then asked what sorts of people dwelled in that damn'd island."—*Rabelais* IV., chap. lxiv.

"IF ever I should betake myself to swearing," says Sir John Hazlewood in the play, "I shall give very little concern to the fashion of the oath. Odd's bodikins will do well enough for me, and lack-a-daisy for my wife." Many other persons have been much of the same mind as this Sir John, and, possessing a certain esteem for the pomp and circumstance of swearing, have been impelled to cherish some curious substitute so that they might still get a little harmless amusement out of the vice. In this way they have contrived so to compound with their consciences as to become swearers in practice without being blasphemers in intention.

The characteristic of this good Hazlewood is his extreme tolerance and neutrality. He is not among the swearers himself, but at a moment of danger he is prepared to join that body, taking service in the ranks. To disown allegiance altogether never for a moment coincides with his sense of the becoming. The worthy man is too loyal to the set rules of his acknowledged leaders, to harbour a notion so subversive and dangerous. And in this particular we shall find he has been followed by the greater number not only of his own degree and class but of all orders and conditions.

A circumstance like this would seem to suggest some remarkable underlying motive as accounting for the wonderful omnipotence of swearing. It is possible that an occult virus congenial to its development is so insinuated into the composition of the human mind as to defy the power of ethics wholly to eradicate it. Can it be that the habit owes its existence and source of delight to some soothing and pleasureful qualities which, like the solace of the tobacco-leaf or the balm of the nightshade, the world will not willingly forego?

We are disposed to think that the instinct of swearing is very deeply rooted in the mental constitution. A very little experience of mankind will incline one to the belief that the censors of morals have on the whole done wisely in temporising with this strange humour. Of all the philosophers who of old laid down rules for worldly guidance, Socrates may be trusted to have held at a just appreciation the trips and sallies of

Athenian manhood. And yet even Socrates is understood to have sworn deeply and volubly. Not, however,
the Herculean oaths that were resounded in the amphi-
theatre and at the festivals, but by the names of more
despicable objects, by the dog, the caper, and the plane-
tree.* The philosopher was too well versed in the ways
of headstrong humanity to run exactly counter to all
the follies inspired by the grape of Chios and Lesbos.
On the contrary, he gains his momentary end and
creates a lasting remonstrance while seemingly sporting
and dallying with the abuse. In like manner, Aristophanes could afford to trifle with the asseverations of
his own Athenian audiences. In portraying the wind-
paved city of the feathered tribes, he transforms these
oaths into the milder shape of "by snares," "by nets,"
"by meshes." And further to display the ludicrous
side of Attic swearing, he records a time when "no
man used to swear by gods, but all by birds. And still
Lampon swears by the goose when he practises any
deceit."†

It would seem almost as if all writers of this indulgent turn had arrived at one perception, namely,

---

* Socrates' oath, *by the cabbage,* μὰ την κραμβην is given in Athenæus,
ib. ix. p. 370.
 . † Aristophanes, 'The Birds.'

that "bad language" is an indispensable element in social life, an element to be only softened by ridicule or perhaps be checked by dissuasion. To seek to suppress it altogether is regarded as futile. The same impression has evidently prevailed among the number of practical philosophers who in everyday life are accustomed to handicap the ebullitions of this impetuous vice. They may place nagging obstacles in the way of its career, and burdens upon its back; but otherwise it is allowed to run its course. By means of an accepted code of rules a kind of *modus vivendi* in this respect is obtained. Thus the conversation that is conceded in a club smoking-room would be intolerable in the boudoir. In some sort men have been permitted the enjoyment of swearing, and that with impunity, provided they did not carry it beyond the prohibited pale. To turn again to ancient Athens for illustration, we find that even children were allowed to swear profanely by the name of Hercules, but with the single restriction that they should do so in the open air. The oath was for some singular reason deemed the especial privilege of young people, and was only thought offensive and visited with punishment when invoked within the curtilage of the dwelling.*

* Plutarch, Quæstion. Rom., p. 271.

It has always seemed to us that vituperative swearing is too closely allied to the passion of animosity to be
ever successfully treated apart from the human failing
from which it takes its rise.   Joy and hatred, terror
and surprise must indeed be very old and steadfast
emotions in the history of the world; and while we
should prefer to find that joy is the more universal
of these perceptions, hatred is, we fear, the more historic
and the more enduring.   Animosity is resolute even
in its caprices; it has few facilities for disguise and
but little capacity for assumption.   The tones and
gestures it employs are perfectly unequivocal, and not
easily mistaken.   For although the vocabulary of
hatred has from time to time received handsome em-
bellishment at the hands of ingenious and illustrious
haters, its wonted expression must always remain fixed.
The keynote is the oath which, in all ages and in all
languages, passion seems to generate with but very
little assistance.

Among a people who, perhaps unjustly, have been
prided for the choiceness of their swearing, the favourite
growth and very spoilt-child of animosity is the word
of an exceedingly forcible kind.   In endeavouring to
chronicle the amenities of the British "damn," we
believe we are dealing with a monosyllable possessing

a remarkable fund of application.   The term has fairly
puzzled the ingenuity of continental neighbours to com-
prehend.   Not only has it excited their ridicule, but we
are not sure that it has not even stimulated their envy.   It
has been said by one of the sprightliest of Frenchmen,
that a foreigner might conveniently travel through
England with the assistance only of this one particle of
speech.

   The uses, or the misuses, of the word would seem to
be twofold : first, as an accessory of abuse, and secondly,
as an accessory of geniality.   In some instances the two
qualities are blended.   Thus the knights of the road
who stopped coaches and filched purses on the heath
of Newmarket or Hounslow usually rode off "damning"
their victims and advising them to sue the hundred for
the injury.   Whereat it was customary to remark, in
the joking spirit of the age, that the villains showed
themselves true men of the law by taking their fee
before they gave their advice.   Everyone who re-
members the eleventh canto of Don Juan will recollect
the pugilistic conflict that took place upon that hero's
first arrival at the outskirts of London, a shower of
blackguard oaths taking a conspicuous part in the
encounter.   Juan, weary with travel, has arrived at
Shooter's Hill.   He is meditating upon the vastness of

the city stretched in panorama at his feet. Suddenly his studious occupation is interrupted by the onset of a 'gang of footpads. In the confusion that ensues, his ignorance of the language places him at a momentary disadvantage. The only English word he is acquainted with being, as he phrases it, "their shibboleth, 'God-damn.'" Even this Juan innocently imagines to be a form of salutation, a sort of God-be-with-you, a misconception which the poet professes to think not unnatural—

> " . . . . for half English as I am
> (To my misfortune) never can I say
> I heard them wish 'God with you,' save that way."

No stanza of the poem is more replete than this with a vein of painfully sarcastic drollery. The insular failing is elsewhere frequently displayed by the poet in the trying light cast from a misanthrope genius.

But perhaps the severest hit, and not the less severe because tempered with banter and good humour, is that which has been directed from the pen of Beaumarchais.* "Diable! c'est une belle langue que l'anglais; il en faut peu pour aller loin; avec Goddam en Angleterre on ne manque de rien. . . . les Anglais à la vérité,

---

* 'Mariage de Figaro,' iii. 5.

ajoutent par-ci par-là quelques autres mots en con-
versant ; mais il est bien aisé de voir que Goddam est
le fond de la langue."

The highest point of wit in this direction must be
supposed to have been reached when Evariste Parny, a
poet of no mean celebrity, produced his "Goddam!
poëme en quatre chants, par un French-dog." This
was in the year XII. or, as we now should prefer to
call it, 1804.

The countrymen, and in one remarkable instance, a
countrywoman of Beaumarchais, have been particularly
industrious in fastening this aspersion upon their
English neighbours. So long ago as 1429, when the
arms of Shrewsbury and Bedford had well-nigh wrested
the last jewel from the diadem of France, and a peasant
maiden of the Calvados had flung herself into Orleans
to stem the tide of the English advance, there likewise
came to the aid of the fainting cause a welcome supply
of mirth and invective. The Maid of Orleans, inspirit-
ing the beleaguered army by harangue, by entreaty,
even by quips and jests, kept them constantly reminded
of the insular nickname. Rising from sleep and putting
on her armour to direct the memorable assault upon the
Tournelles, a soldier of her command ventured to produce a repast of fish, and prayed her to break her fast.

"Joan, let us eat this shad-fish before we set out."
The Maid indignantly put aside the proffered gift,
" In the name of God" said she, " it shall not be eaten
till supper, by which time we will return by way of the
bridge, and I will bring you back a Goddam to eat it
with." How the redoubtable Tournelles was taken by
steel and culverin, and how Joan succeeded in bringing
back many hundred Goddams, has become matter of
history. As to the conclusion of the Maid's career,
there has been opened a wide field of controversy, but
one incident in the closing chapter of her life is sup-
ported by reliable testimony. While undergoing close
imprisonment pending the decision of her fate, two
English noblemen, the Earls of Warwick and Stafford,
came to visit her in gaol, and would seem to have held
out hopes of ransom; Joan, irritated at the specious
language of her visitors, retorted on them sharply : "I
know you well," she cried, " you have neither the will
nor the power to ransom me. You think when you
have slain me, you will conquer France ; but that you
will never bring about. No! although there were one
hundred thousand Goddams in this land more than
there are!" *

* MS. Bibliothèque nationale. ' Collection Complète des Mémoires,'
vol. viii.

With the assumption of the soldier's tunic, it did not follow that she adopted the manners of the military fire-eater, or suited herself to the wild talk of camps. The epithet "Goddam" in the mouth of La Pucelle was expressive only of acrimony towards the oppressor, and even assuming it to have been irreverent and ungainly, was not the least in accord with the language that usually distinguished her. So far from condoning the irregularities of military life, Joan seems to have laid her strongest commands upon the soldiery to abstain from oath-taking, and in one instance would appear to have made a convert of an illustrious kind. Stories are told, which we need not here repeat, of the licence in expression of the celebrated La Hire, who may be likened to a Boanerges among swearers. With him the habit was perfectly indispensable. At last Joan came to a compromise. He was to retain to the full his privilege of swearing, provided he referred in his oaths to no other substantive than his marshal's baton, and thenceforward this sturdy soldier betook himself to this emasculated form of swearing.

According to an authority that is entitled to credit, a very similar subterfuge would seem to have been attempted at a still earlier period of French history. The courtiers of Louis IX. were wont to indulge in what may be described as a very flippant and volatile description of swearing. The indignation of their master, the beloved St. Louis, may of itself have been no inconsiderable punishment, but a still worse one was provided in the statute-book, which prescribed the penalty of branding the tongue with a red-hot iron upon every commission of the offence. The oaths which at this period were the cause of the greatest mortification to the saintly king were the *cordieus*, the *têtedieus*, the *pardieus* and the numerous offshoots, the effigies of which still survive in the pages of Rabelais and Molière— the 'Moyen de Parvenir' and the 'Baron de Fœneste.' With the airy nonchalance of practised sophistry, these apologists of swearing conceived a device that to themselves at least proved eminently satisfactory. At this time there was at the palace a pet dog, known by the name of Bleu. To elude the harsh sentence of the law that might for ever deprive these gay swearers of the power of taking oaths, they determine to substitute for *dieu* the name of the favourite dog. Thus *cordieu* became CORBLEU and *têtedieu* became TÊTEBLEU, and so on throughout the entire series. Unlike the rigid St. Louis, a later French monarch, Henry IV. was himself a notorious offender in this respect. On every occasion of annoyance, he was heard to give utterance to his favourite oath "Jarnidieu!" To him once came his confessor, Coton. "Sire," said the confessor, "it is a great sin to mention the holy name in these terms." "You are right," said Henry, "in future I will say 'Jarnicoton.'"

It is singular to turn for a moment from the extravagant exuberance of a polished French court to find the same device existing in a very different era of the world's history. The educated Athenian vented his "Mon Dieus" like any Frenchman on the boulevard, and in like manner learned to soften his "Μὰ τὸν θεὸν" to a simple "Μὰ τὸν" in deference to ears polite. Socrates himself, never altogether free from a predilection for jocose forms of swearing, also took the palace dog, so to speak, as his colloquial stalking-horse, and, like the courtiers of St. Louis, swore νὴ τον κύνα.

The framework of the story dealing with the conversion of La Hire has not been lost upon the writers of the theatre. A *petite comédie* well known on the boards of the Théâtre Français as 'Les Jurons de Cadillac,' is occupied with the sufferings of a naval officer who is constrained by feminine influence to relinquish his customary expletives. "How is it," asks La Comtesse, "that you have contracted this horrible habit; you, a scion of an old stock, one of our first

Gascon gentlemen?" Cadillac's answer is spirited. "Comtesse, I was brought up by my grandfather, an old sea-dog, corbleu! With him I learnt to swear before I learnt to read, and if he has not taught me the language of courts, it is because, sacrébleu! he did not know it. He made me a true sailor, ventre mahon!" The Comtesse insists that, as a proof of the captain's professions of regard, he should abstain from indulging in this habit for the space of one single hour. Should the ordeal be successfully passed, she consents that he shall receive her hand as his reward. Cadillac is fairly driven to desperation. "Ask of me anything but that!" he exclaims; "only let me swear, or I shall go mad!" Finally he sees no help for it but to accept the challenge, and the audience is detained in a state of amusing suspense while witnessing the contrivances with which the honest captain endeavours to overcome the difficulty. He tampers with the hands of the clock in the hope of abridging the hour of trial, and this ruse being discovered he unworthily seeks safety in sullen silence. "No, no, captain," objects the Comtesse, "unless you converse it is not fair play." His tormentor lures him with all her skill to let slip one of his unpremeditated expletives, and a hundred times the worthy fellow is on the point of giving way. At last, beguiled into a description of one of his most thrilling sea-fights, and with the recollection of the wild scenes of carnage passing vividly before his eyes, he is no longer able to maintain composure. He bursts into a volume of his old sea terms, but the lady, moved, as it would seem, by the *élan* and spirit of the recital, finds it in her heart to be merciful. The play concludes with a modest *sacrébleu*, this time spoken by La Comtesse. It will be seen from the evidence of this performance alone that in ascribing to our nationality a monopoly of energetic language, public report has hardly been discriminating.

Not desiring, however, to turn the tables upon our aspersers, we propose to still further pursue the fortunes of the Britannic shibboleth from when we left it upon the lips of La Pucelle. The aspersion cast upon the English on the Picard battle-fields continued to be handed down in camp story and in rugged *vaux-de-vire*. Neither did it cease to provoke derision and merriment when it had entered into the common parlance of the Paris cabaret, and became the stock property of the Palais Royal farce.* The " Goddam " that

---

* " *Williams.* Ah, damnation ! Goddam !
    Blondel. Goddam ! Monsieur est Anglais apparemment."
                                        ' *Cœur de Lion,*' 1789.

greeted British officers rollicking through the city of pleasure in the days succeeding Waterloo was the same term of opprobrium that assailed the English archers at Agincourt and Honfleur.

To what "mute inglorious" satirist we are indebted for this lasting compliment we shall probably never now determine. The word is at least discovered in the collection of Norman ballads subjoined to the ' Vaux-de-Vire' of Master Oliver Basselin published at Caen, 1821. This work dates from the early part of the sixteenth century, but has reference to the events of the preceding one. It more particularly speaks of Henry V. as dying *par le mal de St. Fiacre* and of Henry VI. as ascending the throne. It is the latter monarch who is referred to in these verses as " little King Goddam "—

> "Ils ont chargé l'artillerye sus mer,
> Force bisquit et chascun ung bydon,
> Et par la mer jusqu'en Biscaye aller,
> Pour couronner leur petit roy godon."

We might search in vain for mention of the expression in English writings of the same period. In France however the epithet is repeated with equal malignancy in the angry verses which Guillaume

Besides the oath of Socrates, "by the dog," he is reported to have sworn variously by the goose and by the plane-tree. Those who argue in favour of the piety of the philosopher, explain that the habit was assumed as a foil to the irreverent mention of the gods that was then so universal. Lucian attaches an intelligible meaning to these flippant expletives, and represents Socrates as justifying their use. "Are you not aware," he is presumed to reason, "that the dog is the Anubis of Egypt, the Sirius of the skies; and in hell is the keeper Cerberus?" and Plutarch is also found to comment on the oath, "those that worship the dog have a certain sacred meaning that must not be revealed; in the more remote and ancient times the dog had the the highest honours paid to him in Egypt." In the copiousness of the ancient swearing the notion of an oath accommodated itself to all the varieties of monstrous gods. The divinities Isis and Osiris were invoked in witness of a sacred pledge no less than the garlic, the leek, and the onion, and indeed every other deity which, as was said by the Roman satirist, grew and flourished in the market-gardens of Alexandria.

We are admitted to a just appreciation of the levity of Athenian swearing through the medium of one of the most remarkable performances ever placed upon the

F

stage, whether of the modern or the ancient world.
When, returning from an expedition, Socrates repaired
to the theatre to witness Aristophanes' comedy 'The
Clouds,' he found himself portrayed upon the scene as
the central figure of the drama. He was even represented swung up in a basket in his own thinking-shop
and giving utterance to innumerable heresies and follies.
When Strepsiades offers to swear by the gods, he is at
once interrupted by Socrates in the basket, who reminds
him that the gods are not current coin in his system of
philosophy. "By what then do you swear?" asks
Strepsiades ; "by the iron money, as they do at Byzan-
tium?" Unhappily the query remained unanswered.

The result, however, of the Socratic influence is intended to be shown by the circumstance of Strepsiades
subsequently swearing "by the mist!" and reproaching
his son for taking oaths in the name of a deity of the
outside world. Presently, on being importuned by a
creditor for the return of twelve minæ lent for the
purchase of a dapple-grey horse, he is ready to swear
any number of oaths "by the gods" that he is innocent
of the debt. His opinions have in the course of this
short dialogue undergone alteration. He feels justified in ridding himself of his obligation to repay the

loan by making use of declarations which the philosopher has argued are no longer of any consequence.

"And will you be willing to deny it upon oath of the gods?" screams the creditor.

"What gods?" asks Strepsiades.

"Jupiter, Mercury, and Neptune."

"Yes, by Jupiter!" rejoins Strepsiades, "and would pay down, too, a three-obol piece besides to swear by them."

It must have been a sorry spectacle to have beheld Socrates in the midst of an Athenian audience solemnly witnessing this masterpiece of buffoonery, and a still sadder one to those whose feeling was still enlisted upon the side of the moribund system of oath-taking.

One singular instance of whimsicality in the ancient practice of swearing must not be allowed to pass unnoticed. The Levantine merchants trading with the port of Rhodes had familiarized Athenian households with a most excellent description of cabbage. The herb was only to be found in its highest perfection upon the southern coasts of the Mediterranean. This Rhodian cabbage had a mellower flavour than that indigenous to the Troad, and was, moreover, prized by all Athenian

topers as the surest antidote to the effects of drink.
No supper-table would have been perfect without some
preparation of this delicacy, and the gay revellers knew,
or in any case imagined, that with this nostrum close
at hand the choicest Chian or Lesbian vintages might
safely be defied.   Hence it was that the very name of
so precious a vegetable came to be held in estimation,
until it was customary to say that if it were permitted
to blaspheme without offending the gods, it would be by
mention of the Rhodian cabbage.*   The lover in a
fragment of the lost poet Ananius invokes it solemnly
in evidence of his attachment, and there is found a
suggestion in the iambics of Hipponax of the vegetable
having even entered into the mythology—

> " He, falling down, worshipped the seven-leaved cabbage,
>   To which, before she drank the poisoned draught,
>   Pandora brought a cake at Thargelia."

This oath by the cabbage became in time the favourite expletive of Ionia, and having winged its way
westwards, still lingers in the shape of the exclamation
Cavolo! as a popular phrase of modern Italy.

Specific forms of swearing were in a great measure

* Letter from Lynceus at Rhodes to Diagoras at Athens, in ' Journal
des Savants,' 1839, p. 37.

localised in the ancient world. As the Thebans swore by Osiris, the Ionians by the cabbage and the colewort, so also in Athens Minerva formed the staple of the national oaths. No Roman citizen was heard to swear by Castor. Why there should have been this denial upon the part of those who swore freely by Pollux is not easily explained. But while the Roman women were loud in the use of " Mecastor "—the affix *me* being supplied to adapt the name to swearing purposes, the men abjured that oath as scrupulously as the women in their turn ignored the expression " Mehercule." * Hercules himself, so the story went, was known to swear but one oath in the whole course of his life. In recognition of such singular forbearance, the Roman children were instructed never to make light use of his sacred name. The prohibition, however, extended no further than the four walls and curtilage of the dwelling, and they were free to make what use they liked of it out of doors.

An instance of oaths being subjected to the like whimsical conditions is noticeable in the domestic manners of Old Germany. We gather from the popular mediæval satire, the 'Ship of Fools,' that a

* Aulus Gellius, xi. 6. We find these oaths so distributed in Terence and Plautus, the women swearing by Castor and the men by Hercules.

code of rules had been formulated regulating the propriety of swearing. Society in this case would seem to have formed its precedents of oath-taking, and to have withheld its sanction from any others than its own. There was a time in Germany it appears when a man adopted an oath as deliberately as he might take to a trade, it being only necessary, to bring it within the licensed pale, that it should be derived from the symbols of his own or his father's occupation. The particular merit of this system was that while it partook of all the abandonment and conferred all the enjoyment of swearing, it was practically no swearing at all. When, in an outburst of passion, the grazier called out upon his beeves, or the smith invoked his anvil or his sledge, all the advantages of swearing, whatever they may be held to be, had been accomplished, and that without prudery being ruffled or innocence shocked. In fact the needs of society had invented a kind of stalking-horse for blasphemy, and the Bob Acreses and Captain Absolutes of that day must have found themselves cruelly hoodwinked by the inanimate effigy of swearing.

But while northern nations were conspicuous for the substantial and ponderous nature of their oaths, the Roman yielded to none in the multiform versatility of his adjurations. Caligula owned a horse that he not only treated as a fellow-being and brought to meals at his table, but whose name served him wherewith to pronounce his accustomed oaths. The same emperor is reported to have put to death a Roman citizen who refused to swear by his "imperial genius." Another of the oaths prescribed by command of Caligula was "per numen Drusillæ." This wretched woman he constrained his subjects to worship as a divinity. To explain this partiality for the use of these absurd if not impious oaths, it would seem that a tradition had been circulated, ascribing the duration of his own lifetime to the period during which the oath should pass current. Any attack of illness that happened to the emperor was directly attributed to the waning popularity of the oath. Nor was the doctrine strange to many of the nationalities over which the Roman sway extended. We have it distinctly occurring among the Scythians,* and it has more recently been noticed by travellers as existing among half-barbarous tribes. The oath itself was probably a development of the affirmation that has been used more than any other in the history of the world. The *life* or the *head* of the ruler of the chief

* Herodotus, bk. iv. 67. It was the *hearth* of kings of Scythia that was dealt with in this way.

tribesman, or of the spiritual prophet, has invariably furnished the true standard of affirmation. But even as a mere domestic oath, the *head* of the goodman of the house seems to have been permitted a degree of solemnity—

     " Per caput hoc juro, per quod pater ante solebat."
              Virgil, Æn. ix. 300.

CHAPTER V.

"He swore by the wound in Jesu's side."—*Coleridge,*
' *Christabel.*'

WE may now turn our backs upon the luxuriant and
fanciful swearing of the ancient world and pursue our
researches into one other division of the subject that
gives rise to more serious reflections. The diversions
of the Roman and the Greek in the way of imprecation
seem to have been mostly intended in good part, and
to have been productive of little theological odium.
But there is a body of swearing that has diffused itself
through Christian countries which is the very reverse
of sportive, and has undeniably provoked the strongest
feelings of aversion. The abuse to which we allude
consisted mainly in the indiscriminate use of popular
oaths that selected the limbs and members of Christ as
the paraphernalia of swearing. There does not appear
at the present day any great irreverence in the exclamation, "S'light," or "S'lid," or "Bodikins," as,
happily, the wave of impiety that brought them has
long since broken and passed away. Indeed, as they

now occur in the pages of sixteenth century writings, they only strike the modern reader in the light of so many interruptions from the text. But we shall find as we pursue the inquiry further, that there was a great deal of meaning wrapped up in these expletives, and that they played a by no means unimportant part in the workings of the mediæval understanding.

Whatever may have been the malignities laid to the charge of the later middle ages, it is certain that the Englishman was on the whole of a reverential type. The pious moralist who laboured in those times was so far assisted by an utter absence of captious criticism to honeycomb his teaching, and by the solid sense of appreciation that was wont to fill the minds of his listeners. He was practised, moreover, in the exercise of two potent influences that he was ever ready to exert. The one may be said to have had its root in his hearers' fund of ready sympathy, the other in their ghostly apprehension of horror and dread. It is not at all surprising that in later times we should find an opaqueness to have obscured the clear crystal of these subtle perceptions, for fear and pity have no longer the same ascendancy in a busy world. But at a period more piously illiterate, things of this shadowy nature were linked very closely to objects of a material kind.

A long process of reasoning could then be saved by reference to some obscure picture of monkish fancy. And so, in the glooms and twilights of mediæval life, the moralist might insure speedy victory by over-whelming men's intellects by an appeal to the formidable images of terror and compassion.

The pre-Reformation Englishman, stricken and toil-worn, having no hope save in forbearance from the skies, and no consolation but in the repose of the ale-house, could yet be awed and subdued by the apprehension of some priest-directed shape of ghostly terrorism. Above all, he had been made to grasp a sentiment, which, slightly as it can be treated in a secular work, may be said to have left no adequate imprint upon the Pro-testant world. By dint of the monastic teaching, he had been brought to entertain a keen personal realisa-tion of the actual sufferings of Christ. The fact is self-evident from every fragment of contemporaneous litera-ture intended to react upon the fears and sympathies of uncultivated men. It was the constant presentment of the notion of the divine agony, the daily calling to remembrance of the thorns, the nails, and the hyssop, that was relied upon to keep alive in these poor agued souls some struggling flame of spiritual vitality. And so surely was the spark wont to kindle, and so reverently was the similitude of these priestly images treasured up, that they formed the mainstay of the ploughman's faith, the sum total of the poor man's theology.

From this cause it arose, as there is now every reason to suspect, that the country was at one time inundated with a torrent of the most acrid and rasping blasphemy. It would not be difficult to trace the relative connection between the luxuriance of oath-taking and the various forms of religion under which oath-taking has successively flourished. It could be shown that the swearing of most Catholic states is of greater fertility, and displays a readier fund of invention than that of countries brought under the reformed faith. The more religion appeals to the senses, the more fecund has been the vocabulary of oaths. The more it has been made the subject of illustration and imagery, the more finished and ornate have been the comminations in use. A priest-ridden nation, such as the Spanish or Italian, has always been eminent for its proficiency in blasphemy; and as part of the argument it may not be out of place to mention the instance of the hedge-parson in the 'Fortunes of Nigel,' who, by reason of his superior knowledge of divinity, could swear with greater volubility than any of his associates.

Thus it was that, labouring under the ban of priestly exaction, and confronted on all sides by the ghostly emblems of wrath and condemnation, there descended upon England in the thirteenth and fourteenth centuries, a torrent of the hardest and direst of verbal abuse. Not mere words of intemperate anger came bubbling to the surface, but sullen and defiant blasphemies, execrations that proclaimed open warfare with authority and a lasting separation from everything that was tender in men's faith. Imprecations were contrived · from every incident in the narrative of the Crucifixion. The limbs and members of the slain Christ were made the vehicle of revolting profanation. The didactic writers of the time, no less than epic poets and sprightly versifiers, give full testimony to the prevalency of the offence. The laureate, Stephen Hawes, Lydgate, Chaucer and the "moral Gower," all are alike loud in their expression of horror and renunciation. Among the later writers replete with instances of the scandal is the epigrammatist, Robert Crowley, who enumerates a lengthy catalogue of expletives current in his day. Although by the time Crowley appeared upon the scene the language of blasphemy had become a little softened by the admixture of rather more innocent particles, as "by cock and pye," or "by

the cross of the mousefoot," the author still finds it
necessary to record a set of hard, grating oaths pronounced by the "hands," the "feet," and the "flesh"
of Christ.

To refer, for instance, to the use of the one word
"zounds!" This strikes us now-a-days as anything
but a very solemn or a very momentous form of adjuration. But in unreformed England—the England that
still adored the *Genetrix incorrupta*, and had earned
among the devout the title of Our Lady's Dower, it
was absolutely impossible to surpass in blasphemy the
hideous import that had been imparted to the user of
the word. It was in fact nothing else than a rebellious
and mutinous rendering of the once sacred oath taken
by the wounds of the Redeemer. There are few who
can probably now realise the conspicuous place then
occupied in the Catholic worship by the legends relating
to the five several incisions in the body of Christ. The
monkish representations of the wounds were depicted in
countless rosaries and Books of Hours. Confraternities
were formed in the Church for their greater veneration. There were occasions when papal absolution was
specially extended to those worshippers who paid their
devotions to the wound in the side of Christ. The so-
called measurement of them was even preserved in

families, and was reputed to be a charm.* In the great
northern insurrection of 1536, known as the Pilgrimage
of Grace, the Five Wounds was the badge under which
York and Lincoln farmers marched to avenge the
spoliation of the monasteries. Such was the oath in the
days of the last King Henry. Its more modern application scarcely requires illustration, but if any such
were needed, we might find it in the villainous lines
which Lord Byron wrote in connection with a certain
trip on board the *Lisbon* packet.

To the present hour, in Italy, the popular oaths
are in close alliance with the Romanist faith. The
ordinary exclamation " *Per l'ostia* " is the equivalent of
" God's bread !" that so long did duty in England of the
pre-Reformation era. A modern traveller has noticed
how distinct an impress has been set upon Italian
swearing by the particular notions of heavenly beings
that are inculcated by the national creed. A workman
in an art-studio was heard vociferating in such terms as
" *Per Christo*," " *Per sangue di Christo*," " *Per mala-
detto sangue di Christo*," whereupon the following conversation occurred :—

---

* For an able article on the Five Wounds as represented in Art, see
Journal of Brit. Arch. Association for Dec. 1874, by the Rev. W.
Sparrow Simpson.

"Do you forget who Christ is, that you thus blaspheme Him?"

"Bah!" replied the man, "I am not afraid of Him."

"Who, then, do you fear?"

"I'm afraid of the Madonna, and not of Him."

The fact was that the Mother of God was the sole being the mind was brought to esteem with feelings of veneration. Christ was only the *bambino*, or infant in arms, and nothing more.*

The state of feeling that still prevails in Italy should go far to explain the presence in pre-Reformation England of this widely-spread body of irreverent swearing. With the Reformation, however, the contagion was shortly to abate. The severer authors at the close of the sixteenth century do not have to complain so bitterly of these jarring elements of vituperation. In the literature of the stage there is a marked improvement: in none but the earlier of the

---

* 'Roba di Roma,' by W. W. Story, 1863. The writer adds, "A curious feature in the oaths of the Italians may be remarked. *Dio mio* is usually an exclamation of sudden surprise or wonder; *Madonna mia*, of pity and sorrow, and *per Christo* of hatred and revenge. It is in the name of Christ, and not of God as with us, that imprecations, curses, and maledictions are invoked. The reason is very simple. Christ is to him the judge and avenger of all, and so represented in every picture he sees, from Orcagna's and Michael Angelo's Last Judgment down, while the Eternal Father is a peaceful old figure bending over him.

Elizabethan comedies do the characters accentuate their meaning by reference to the grossest description of blasphemy. When expletives occur they are generally in the spirit of derision and lampoon. As the writings of the stage grew more robust, the custom altogether wore away. It may, indeed, be held that the subversion of the Catholic religion was mainly, if not entirely, accountable for the change. There is certainly a marked distinction between the oaths of the outgoing and incoming creeds. But if we have been finally spared from the ravages of the infection, we may attribute our deliverance to that reserve of reverence of which we have spoken as possessed by English laymen, and to the pious devices that were practised upon it by the inferior orders of preachers.

The position they chose to assume in combating this " fine old gentlemanly vice " is a singular feature in its history. Their method was to associate the practice of swearing with the notion of actual bodily pain being occasioned to the Saviour. They made it appear that Christ in person was put to extreme physical agony on every occasion of its committal. Not alone did they assert the wantonness and hardihood of so directly incurring the Divine displeasure, but they raised the most piteous appeal to the compassion of

G

these benighted swearers. It was daily proclaimed from their pulpits that the profanity in this one respect of professedly Christian men had worked a sharper and more agonising martyrdom than that formerly designed by the Jews themselves. In countless broadsheets, no less than by pictorial illustration, the wounds of Christ were portrayed as hourly re-opened, and the sufferings of Golgotha renewed from day to day. The doctrine gained additional credit when transferred from the hands of monkish authors and embraced by popular and captivating pens. Stephen Hawes, own poet to carpet-knights and buckram soldiery, brought home conviction to a class of offenders that a whole con- sistory would not have succeeded in convincing. In a rhyming pamphlet, prefaced by a figure of the bleeding Christ, Hawes depicts with awful realism those suffer- ings which, as he believed, were being actually and bodily inflicted.* The author of 'Bel Amour' describes the feet and hands of Christ as literally pierced anew, and every member torn and lacerated by reason of the imprecations of unheeding Christians.

At this time of day it might be difficult to ascertain with any certainty the origin of this forced view of the iniquity of swearing. So far as concerns printed

* 'The Conversyon of Swerers,' 1540.

literature, we discover it for the first time in the
doggerel of the poet Hawes, but it is none the less
traceable to that encyclopædic work of the thirteenth
century, the ' Miroir du Monde.' This takes us to the
year 1279, and instances could be furnished showing
its regular passage through the next three centuries,
until the monkish notion is at last surrendered and
delivered over to the cleansing fires of the Reformation.
The last of the English authors who seems to have
seriously advanced the theory is to be found in the ·
rigid disciple of asceticism, Thomas Becon.

Becon was a man who, throughout a devout and
severe life, had set himself sternly to the task of
rebuking the immoderate lawlessness of the orders
among which he lived. The rustic usage of collecting
round the village tavern to celebrate the Sabbath in
sport and holiday was one particularly repellant to the
mind of Becon, and held by him to be the mainspring
of all the evils that ravaged the country-side. The
fore part of the day having been devoted to the services
of the Church, it was usual for a time of high festival
to succeed the morning's austerities. Noon discovered
all the grown men of the village assembled round the
vintner's door and partaking of the ale-house hospi-
talities. Here feats of rude strength were performed,

wrestlers practised their throws, and sturdy fellows played bouts at quarter-staff. ₁ Foot-races were run upon the greensward for wholesome wagers of barley-cake, and games of hazard were conducted under the shelter of the ivy-bush at the publican's threshold. Bets were staked, dice were rattled, and yokels learned to place the dues of the harvest-field upon the fortunes of the winning or losing colour. When, therefore, after earnest and fruitless entreaty, the good Becon rushed into print and produced his learned 'Invective,' he did not omit to visit with uncompromising censure the chartered licence of this Sunday festival.

The riot and pastime that on every seventh day had been wont to disturb the quietude of rustic life appeared to our reformer as a direct encouragement to the practice of swearing, and in fact as constituting so many training-schools for the cultivation of this unwelcome accomplishment. In the hope of rendering the habit positively forbidding to the more impressionable among his readers, he reminds them how the body of the Saviour is actually torn and mangled by reason of the imprecations hurled at him in these country sports. Oaths, he deplores, were then used in every matter of chopping and changing, of bargaining and selling,

and he groans to think how the "dicer" will swear
rather than passively submit to the loss of a single
cast, the "carder will tear God in pieces rather than
lose the profit of an ace."

It is a feature that must be very palpable to the
student of incipient literature, that when once an
original and daring notion was fairly launched upon
the world, it was not allowed to founder for want of
repetition. The peculiar mode of thought which we
have ventured to ascribe to the 'Miroir du Monde' in
the thirteenth century, could boast a long line of
exponents in the interval that closed with Thomas
Becon. The writer to whose industry, rather than
invention, English laymen were indebted for their
acquaintance with this painful doctrine was a certain
Dan Michael, described as a brother of the Cloister
of Saint Austin. This person has produced a didactic
treatise based upon the model of the famous 'Miroir,'
an original from which no writer at that time felt
himself justified in departing. With the subject of
swearing he deals in a way that is highly painstaking.
Not to mention the intricate distinctions which he
treats under these several heads, we find that he has
grouped the offences of the tongue into no less than
eight cardinal·divisions. It may be curious to record

the titles as our author enumerates them, notwithstand-
ing that it is scarcely to our purpose to follow him
through the niceties he has created. The branches of
the subject, according to his classification, would therefore seem to be: "ydelnesse," "yelpinge," "bloudynge,"
"todiazinge," "stryfinge," "grochynge," "wypston-
dinge," and lastly "blasfemye." So far as we have
mastered the system of Dan Michael we are driven to
the conclusion that the practice of swearing, as understood in the Cloister of Saint Austin, was, save for the
outward distinction of dress, much the same as prevails
in the later world. "For there are some," says he
of the cloister, "so evil taught that they are able
to say nothing without swearing. Some swear as
if smitten with sudden pain. Others swear by the
sun, the moon, by the head, or by their father's
soul."

Minute as is Dan Michael in his treatment of the
subject of abuse, his elaborations are possibly surpassed
by the next competitor for moralistic fame. Robert of
Brunné, who produced a similar work in the year 1303,
availed himself largely of the other's labours, while he
enriched his collections with recitals of wrong-doing
from his own exclusive stores. From the "Handlyng
Sinne," as the production. is called, one may gather

considerable insight into the state of prejudice existing
at the time. The neighbours tell one another good
stories in church time, and inquire during the sermon
where they can get the best ale. The monks have
become so luxurious that they refuse to shave their
heads and have commenced to array themselves in fine
clothes. The king's courts are crowded with supplica-
ting suitors, craving for redress from the extortions of
trustees and executors, and yielding themselves victims
to the falsity of the men of law. Swearing, at that
time, would seem to be no longer the prerogative of
laymen, but even to have become the privilege of
learned clerks.

To depict what, from this author's point of view,
were the fruits and consequences of blasphemy, Brunné
enters into a narrative describing the Mother of God
presenting the bleeding Jesus to the gaze of the rich
man Dives. The latter inquires the reason for the
Child being gashed with wounds. In reply the Virgin
points out in terms of keen resentment the injuries
inflicted upon the Infant by the swearing of Dives and
his associates. The doctrine of the 'Miroir' is then
introduced in full to demonstrate the infamy and
inhumanity of the practice, the whole concluding with
a promise of repentance on the part of the sinful man.

This fable is only one among many others that were narrated with a view to curbing the propensities of blaspheming swearers. The work that contains it met with general circulation at the commencement of the fourteenth century, but that the spread of the iniquity was not sensibly abated we may infer from other sources of information we have mentioned.* In 1544, the evil was set forth in the light of a national grievance, and was paraded in a broadsheet published in that year entitled a " Supplycacion to Kynge Henry the Eyght."

Such, then, was the ponderous metal that passed current as the swearing of pre-Reformation England. These verbal projectiles were sometimes moulded, how-

---

* The identity of ideas that we have referred to as invariably occurring in mediæval writings, whenever they happen to turn upon a similar theme, may be shown by comparison of the following extracts. They are taken from writers of different times and countries, and who are not directly plagiarising one another. Dan Michael, in the ' Ayenbite of Inwyt' (modernised), has :—

" These (Christians) are worse than the Jews that did crucify him. They broke none of his bones. But these break him to pieces smaller than one doth swine in butchery."

Robert of Brunné, in the 'Handlyng Sinne,' writes :—

> " Thy oaths do him more grievousness,
> Than all the Jews' wickedness ;
> They pained him once and passed away,
> But thou painest him every day."

Again, in the ' Moralité des Blasphémateurs ' (circa 1530) :—

> " Tu luy fais plus dure bataille
> Que les juifz sans nulla faille
> Qui pour toy le crucifierent."

ever, of a lighter calibre, and when employed in the
talk of priests or women, were so nicely rounded off
as to incur little of theological displeasure. Chaucer's
people, in particular, are very punctilious in the propriety of their oaths; good Sir Thopas swearing mildly
"by ale and bread," and Madame Eglantine naming
holy Saint Eligius as the patron of her vows—

> "There was also a nonne, a prioresse,
>   That of hire smyling was ful symple and coy,
>   Hire grettest oath was but by St. Eloy."

In much the same way did princes and dignitaries
of the land single out some swearing cognizance that
might befriend them in the everlasting conflict between
lies and honesty. Edward I. sanctified his oaths by the
mention of a brace of milk-white swans, and whoever
will consult St. Palaye will find that the peacock and
the pheasant entered largely into the codes of chivalry
as bearing witness to the truth of a statement.
Edward III. followed the lead of his grandsire in the
selection of his gage of testimony. At the festival held
in 1349 to celebrate the creation of the Order of the
Garter, his cognizance was the swan, adorned, moreover, with the swearing motto: "Haye! Haye! the
Whyte Swan! by Godde's soule I am thy man."

The tradition that St. Paul was the saint that

Richard III. was wont to conjure with, has found
expression in the tragedy of Shakespeare. Faithful to
the popular notions of the usurper's characteristic, this
form of oath has been placed upon Gloucester's lips at
each impassioned outburst. Henry V., in his wooing
of Katherine, gallantly invokes St. Denis to aid him
in his attempts at love-making. But the chronicler
who seems positively to have had an affection for the
oaths the memory of which he is recalling, is the
historian Brantôme. Upon this unimpeachable testimony we learn that the oath of Louis XI. was *par
la Pâque Dieu,* an affirmation that Scott avails himself of in his portraiture of that monarch in ' Quentin
Durward.' This was succeeded by the *jour de Dieu*
of Charles VIII.; by the *diable m'emporte* of Louis
XII., and the *foi de gentilhomme* of Francis I.
Among the Gascon oaths of Henry IV. the most usual
was *ventre Saint Gris.* As for Charles IX., adds
Brantôme, he swore in all fashions, and always like a
sergeant who was leading a man to be hanged.*

---

* A certain delight in arranging the favourite oaths of his contemporaries and of other historical personages is plainly to be seen in
Brantôme. In the ' Vies des Grands Capitaines' he throws off a whole
string of these cherished devices. "On appeloit ce grand capitaine,
Monsr. de la Trimouille, ' La vraye Corps Dieu ' d'autant que c'estoit
son serment ordinaire, ainsin que ces vieux et anciens grands capitaines
en ont sceu choisir et avoir aucuns particuliers à eux ; comme Monsr.

The question has frequently been asked who was
intended by the cognomen Saint Gris? The answer
accorded by Le Duchat, a savant learned in such
matters, is that Saint Francis d'Assise was the person
indicated. It is true that Saint Francis was *ceint* by a
hempen girdle, and, moreover, was clad in a habit of
gris. But there nevertheless seems no reason to suppose that any individual personage was suggested, or,
indeed, as has been stated, that the oath was of a
Huguenot character. Says M. Charles Rozan,* who
has had occasion to refer to this subject, Saint Gris is
purely a creature of fancy, and was constituted a patron
of drinkers, as St. Lâche was a patron of idlers and
St. Nitouche of hypocrites.

The oath of William Rufus, *per vultum de Lucca*,
has raised conjectures as to its probable signification.
The literal meaning, "by Saint Luke's face," being
rejected as not very intelligible, there remain two
distinct explanations: one that it referred to the face
of Christ as painted by St. Luke, the other that the

---

de Bayard juroit, 'Feste Dieu, Bayard!' Monsr. de Bourbon, 'Saincte
Barbe!' le prince d'Orange, 'Saincte Nicolas!' le bonne homme M. de
la Roche du Maine juroit 'Teste de Dieu pleine de reliques!' (où diable
alla il chercher celuy là) et autres que je nommerois, plus sangreneux
que ceux là."

* Ch. Rozan, 'Petites Ignorances de la Conversation.'

portrait of Christ as preserved in the cathedral church
at Lucca is the object intended. To support the first
derivation, credence must be given to the legend which
places the apostle among the artist craftsmen of Judæa,
and has enshrined him as the patron saint of all
workers in the arts. On the other hand, there has reposed for some centuries at Lucca a miraculous crucifix,
famous alike for the marvels it has seen and accomplished. The Tuscan people set great store by the
possession of this relic, and have engraved a representation of it upon their coins. The inscription upon the
Tuscan florin, " Sanctus vultus de Lucca," would seem,
therefore, to be identical with the expletive of William
Rufus.

We have seen how the occupants of the throne have
usually comported themselves in the matter of oaths, but
there is one recorded instance of Plantagenet royalty
having created a singular precedent. If any man can
be said to have ever had cause for swearing, Henry VI.
might be described as being that individual. It is
stated, however, by contemporaries who had opportunities for conversing with this king, and by whom it is
given as a somewhat remarkable fact, that he was never
known to swear under the greatest provocation.

The adage that enjoins us to repeat "no scandal

about Queen Elizabeth" should dispose us to deal lightly with any verbal excesses committed by the virgin queen. It would appear, however, that the moral atmosphere of her court, despite the intellect and talent that adorned it, was not so refined or particular but that the sovereign and the ladies over their breakfasts of steaks and beer could ring out exclamations that to a later generation might appear of rather an astounding character.* To turn for comparison to the era of the next female majesty, it is questionable whether even Sarah Jennings, with all her power of abuse, would not have taken exception to the flavour of some of the Elizabethan adjectives.

A story is told of Edward VI., that at the time of arriving at the kingly dignity he gave way to a torrent of the most sonorous oaths. The pastors and masters charged with the well-being of the royal youth could not but stare in blank astonishment at the conduct of one so well nurtured as the child of Anne Boleyn. It transpired, however, that the young king had been given to believe by one of his associates that language

---

* "A shocking practice seems to have been rendered fashionable by the very reprehensible habit of the Queen, whose oaths were neither diminutive or rare, for it is said that she never spared an oath in public speech or private conversation when she thought it added energy to either."—*Drake, 'Shakspeare and his Times,'* ii. 160.

of the kind was dignified and becoming in the person
of a sovereign. Edward was asked to name the pre-
ceptor who had so ably supplemented the course of the
royal education. This he instantly and innocently
did, and was not a little surprised at the severe whip-
ping that was administered to the delinquent.*

The predicament in which the royal child was placed
is similar to that which once befel a clerical gentleman
while travelling on mule-back across Syria. The
Syrian muleteers are, it seems, accustomed to urge
onward their beasts with the shout of "Yullah!" or
"Bismillah!" and it was under the escort of these
shouting and belabouring drivers that the traveller made
his way into the town of Beyrout. His friends natu-
rally inquired of him what progress he had made in
Arabic, and in reply he told them he had only acquired
two words, *bakhshish* for a present, and *Yullah!* for
go-ahead. He was asked if he had used the latter word
much on his way. Certainly, he said, he had used
it all the way. "Then, your reverence," replied his
friend, "you have been swearing all the way through
the Holy Land."

* J. G. Nicholls, 'Literary Remains of Edward VI.'

CHAPTER VI.

"When a gentleman is disposed to swear, it is not for any standers-by to curtail his oaths."—'*Cymbeline*,' ii. 1.

IN the study of antiquity there are steep and irregular by-paths that defy the traveller every step that he pursues them. It is in threading these tortuous wind-ings that many a fearless venturer has lost foot-hold and been utterly cast away. Many a man with the passion for antiquity deep at his heart, and with limbs well girded to attain to the summit of his aim, has been fain to settle down, jaded and dispirited, at mid-task. He has accomplished nothing perhaps beyond the mere reading of an inscription or deciphering of a medallion, but the spirit of his insight is dimmed and stricken in the work. Thus has it been with many generations of seekers and inquirers. The *virtuosi* and *cognoscenti*, the curious in gems and medals, in brasses and torsos, the commentators and concordancers,—all these may be said to be nothing more than so many units in the lost tribe of eager scholarship. Starting confident of probing to the very source and mystery of things, they have rather preferred the shelter of some attainable evening refuge than be overtaken in their task by the chills and storms of night.

It is easier far, means not being wanting, to place in one's cabinet some matchless group of Capo di Monti, some priceless specimen of the fabric of Sèvres or Dresden, than to tax one's strength in extracting the lessons conveyed by form and colour. It is a simpler matter to be the possessor of Damascus sword-blades or Aleppo prayer-rugs than to burden one's self with reflections upon oriental chivalry or mysticism. And so, again, it is a far readier, as it is certainly a rougher, way of being in sympathy with antiquity, to notch off a fragment in the Acropolis, or carve one's name among the ruins of the Forum, than to originate such poetic passages as Byron uttered over the field of Marathon, or Longfellow in the market-place of Nuremburg. Say what we will, both forms of veneration arise alike from the same innate craving to grasp some part or parcel of the tissue of the past.

To the untiring few who have overcome the drought and dust of the up-land journey, the summit, once attained, will disclose many a point and promontory unsuspected by the purblind dweller in the plain.

The retrospect will reveal to them a busy, thronging life underlying the serenity of history. They will be able to range the perished multitudes in their once motley grouping, to restore warmth and colour to lineaments long obscured in death, and greed and alacrity to the sunk eyes and folded hands. To those whom the spirit of the past is apt to visit as a passionate inspiration, the mere record of consecutive events is often wearisome. It is not altogether for this that they have laboured to catch some murmur, however slight, of the infinite harmony that is being sounded by all the chords of history. Rather, it is to tramp mistily along from generation to generation in the long, forced march of human life. Rather, to probe to the depths of some one of the world's stupendous follies, of some one of its golden vanities, that they have thus cast about them with measure and lead-line. And when they have completely searched out and written of the world's stupendous follies, they will perhaps have written what alone would be worth calling its history.

As some small, tentative contribution to the understanding of this under-life, the plan of this volume has been designed. The past has come down to us cloaked and shrouded, and attended by its decorous retinue of mutes and bearers. We are continually seeking to

H

revive this dead past, just as it was, when its future was a wild, inscrutable thing, and its life was so fragrant, so masterful, and so momentous. It wants a great mental effort to recall events that are as indubitably past as if they had never happened at all. The pleasure of possessing, or of even entering, the vanished territory is a privilege so rare, that there are permitted but a few moments for its enjoyment. It is so subtle a perception that even seasoned historians seldom have the power of imparting it. They may surround us with the conflict of contending legionaries, until we seem to recognise the thud of advancing battalions and the clash and impact of the squadron. These, however lifelike, are impressions of a much grosser and more tangible nature, and can have but little in common with the blended sweetness and irony that pertain to the spontaneous realisation of the dead past.

What we are for ever craving to learn is something more of the gambols, the humours, and the anticing of this sad army, for ever on the march. We yearn to know something more of the vanity and the pettiness, the fever and the longing, of those weary men and women, the memorial of whose lives has been trampled out. The historian will sometimes rend away the veil

that separates us from this unwritten history; but
more often it is the creation of the romancer that helps
to clothe the dim spirit of the past from the loom of its
misty memories; Pascarel, depicting the splendours of
the artist-life of Florence, while Arlecchino and the
rest of the gay carnival troupe are romping in the
faded street of the stocking-makers; Slender and
Shallow and the simple folk of the Cotswold country
ambling out their jests midst the turmoil of those
stirring Lancastrian times; or "sweet Anne Page,"
provoking and winning, three hundred years ago, in
the glades of Windsor Forest. The honest yeoman
who fought the master of fence—three veneys for a
dish of stewed prunes; the foolish justice who in the
days of his youth had beat Sampson Stockfish behind
Gray's Inn, and had heard the chimes at midnight,
lying out in the windmill in St. George's Fields—these
and many kindred types represent to us so many
factors in that progidious army of the unknown that is
never permitted us more thoroughly to know. It is
indeed in the fancy of Shakespeare that this bygone
sweetness and irony seem the oftener to be kindled and
awakened. Not, certainly, in the wordy warring of
Capulet and Montagu; not, perhaps, in the outspoken
chivalry of "Harry the King," or the blunt generosity of

H 2

Falconbridge. But we find it moving and thrilling in every tone caught up from the English country-side, in the echoes wafted from the vintage-lands of France, or the garden walks of Padua. And freshest and daintiest of all, we find it in the poet's snatches of song and rugged bursts of minstrelsy. This indeed is the enchantment that subdues us as the dimpled page advances to the gay theatre lights, and pleading the woes of three hundred years ago, and exhorting now as he exhorted then, bids "Sigh no more, ladies; ladies, sigh no more." It is this which captivates as the scene pauses and the drama halts, that the eye may be carried back through a vista of three centuries to dwell upon a simple "lover and his lass" as they wander "between the acres of the rye."

The subject of swearing the writer has come to regard as one of the many indices by which the paths of our ancestors may be traced. Holding in fitting estimation the monuments of their industry and their prudence, none the less may we seek to view the departed generations in their hours of carelessness and frolic, and may peer into their casinos and their tiring-rooms, their spital-houses and their bridewells. What manner of men were they? we ask. Were they sparkling and festive, tellers of rare stories, dealers

in racy jokes? Were they wholesome in their
living, manly and courageous in their lives, or
were they loose and liquorish, winking at falsehood
and cajoling the truth? And if the monumental
record of their virtues be a just one, why did
they heirloom on posterity this bitter heritage of
swearing?

The truth would seem to be that in every society
there has existed a certain *corps d'élite*, which, distinguished at once by its breeding and its brusquerie,
has perversely thought fit to adopt the insignia of
swearing as its own particular device. In advancing
this explanation of the fidelity with which posterity
has exercised its watchfulness over the bequest of
swearing, we must not for a moment be misunderstood.
It is far from our purpose to associate good breeding
with the use of coarse vituperation, but at the same
time it is impossible to overlook the fact that swearing
has mostly owed its favour and its audacity to the
practice of really cultivated men. The first contrivers
of our modern methods of swearing took pains to raise
an air of mystery and exclusiveness around their
favourite art. "To be an accomplished gentleman,"
says Carlo Buffone, in Ben Jonson's comedy,* "have

* 'Every Man out of his Humour,' i. 1.

two or three peculiar oaths to swear by that no man else swears"; and it would seem to have been one of the gravest charges brought against the Hectors and Bobadils of the Elizabethan stage, that they dare assume acquaintance with courtly oaths. Even Hotspur is portrayed by the dramatist as a most precise and scrupulous swearer. It may be seen how he reproaches Lady Percy for swearing "like a comfit-maker's wife," and bids her "swear me, Kate, like a lady as thou art!" and not to mince her oaths like some city madam or seller of gingerbread.* For upwards of two centuries, the notion of finish and exclusiveness in oath-taking afforded constant merriment for the stage, the creations of the playwright seldom failing to give full scope to the illustration of this strange humour. Every period brought its particular oath and fresh generations of exponents. Now it was the soldier of fortune returned from encounters with the Spaniards or the Turk. Anon it was the tavern rake of King James' day, and after some interval, the wits and foplings of the Restoration. By-and-by, there followed the crowd of nabobs and parvenus, the blustering swearers of the days of East

* 1 Henry IV., iii. 7.

Indian speculation, and finally came the truculent swabbers and commodores of Adelphi melodrama. The *nouveau riche* of the younger Colman, who fails to enrobe himself with dignity by the aid of all ordinary resources, is enjoined by his more practical helpmate to vent his "zounds" and "damme," in emulation of the swearing of the great.

For this *corps d'élite* of which we have spoken have drawn to themselves men the most worthless, and men the most admirable. It has found disciples in every capital—the easy, the affluent, the voluptuous, cheery and sunny of speech, bold and swarthy of countenance. There are numbered among them free livers and free lances innumerable. There are men remarkable for their stores of boisterous animalism, no less than delicate scholars remarkable only for the brightness of their fancy and the vividness of their dreams. They have ever been a composite and a cosmopolitan crew, some shouldering into the ranks by the weight of their purses, or the length of their rent-rolls, others by skill evinced at high midnight, when taper-lights throw pale vertical rays upon a refreshing margent of green cloth. Among them, too, are stout soldiers, bold fearless riders, the wild and fevered blood of many countries, the fervour of Italy, and the craft of the Levant. To the precincts of this gilded and splendid society come many sorts and conditions of aspirants. The boy-parson lays down the sanctity of the priesthood and rapturously sues for admission. Elders of threescore demand an entrance upon the strength of *risqué* stories sprung from garrison-towns and college common-rooms. Skilled physicians feign indifference to their calling that they may smack of the kennel and the hunting-field. Staid, contemplative men, men with a prayer and a tune in them, press into this joyous throng, eager to clasp the bruised fruit of human desire and to claim kindred with these cheery fellowships. But, however varied the elements of the order, the members are constituted alike in this: they are hearty and laughter-loving; they are jolly and courageous.

With outposts so widely distributed, it is the more necessary that there should be some unmistakable uniform, that whether it be in a Paris ordinary, or on the steppes of Tartary, one may easily recognise the scion of the order. Such a uniform, so at least we are constrained to understand it, has, for the most part, been supplied by a subdued and discriminate use of the materials of swearing. A Sandwich Islander appreciates this when he salutes a British crew in terms compounded of oaths and ribaldry.* He is really intending to denote his sense of the distinction of the exalted visitors, when he exclaims: "Very glad see you! Damn your eyes! Me like English very much. Devilish hot, sir! Goddam!" It is to claim kindred with the brotherhood that swell surgeons vent their "blasted!" and "damnation!" as they tender to the ailments of rackety young patients. It is to bridge over the gulf between carelessness and propriety that even mild college tutors will sometimes venture upon a modest "botheration!" or "confounded!" The most fertile and most voluminous swearer, we have been given to understand, exists in the person of one of the leading *littérateurs* of the century when desiring to curry favour with a company of fast men.

Not that it can be altogether denied that there are other contrivances whereby the members of the fraternity succeed in courting mutual recognition. The topic of sporting is, perhaps, the most effectual of these, and it must be understood that a man's convivial condition is often undergoing a crucial investigation when he is questioned as to his views upon such subjects as the Cesarewitch or the Cambridgeshire. The

* See Capt. Basil Hall's 'Fragments of Voyages and Travels, chap. xvi. p. 89.

several processes of swearing would seem however to supply the readiest hall-mark, and are rather of an easier manipulation. This theory of indulgence might go far to explain the leniency of men like Jonathan Swift towards a custom which, had they wished it, they might have deposed from its high places by their ridicule. Swearing was far from being a rock of offence to the society of Harley and St. John. Why else, again, has it been permitted from commanders of the stamp of Picton in the field, and from lawyers of the pattern of Thurlow on the woolsack? "I will now proceed to my seventh point," pursued Sir Ilay Campbell, arguing an interminable Scotch appeal in the House of Lords. "I'm damned if you do," shrieked Lord Thurlow, and the House adjourned neither angry or scandalised. And again, how else explain the exuberance of the Duchess of Marlborough's language when calling at Lord Mansfield's lodgings? His lordship, as we know, was away, and on his return questioned the doorkeeper as to the name of his visitor. "I do not know who she was," replied the man, "but she swore like a lady of quality."

Of Thurlow it has been said that he was renowned as a swearer even in a swearing age. "He took it as a lad who wishes to show that he has arrived at man's

estate. He could not have got on without it." * At one
time a dispute was pending as to the right to present to
a vacant benefice. A certain bishop who claimed the
right sent his secretary to argue with Lord Thurlow,
who, for his part, obstinately maintained the counter-
claim of the Crown. The envoy no sooner opened his
case and made known his message, than Thurlow cut
short all further argument. "Give my compliments
to his lordship, and tell him I will see him damned
before he present." "That," remonstrated the secretary, "is a very unpleasant message to deliver to a
bishop." "You are right," replied Thurlow, "so it is.
Tell him I will see myself damned before he present."

Another professor in the same uncompromising school .
of hard swearers would seem to have been Sir Thomas
Maitland, His Majesty's Lord High Commissioner
administering the government of the Ionian Islands,
at that time and long afterwards under the British
dominion. Sir Charles Napier relates that on arriving
at Corfu to enter upon a military appointment, and
. being ushered into his Excellency's presence, he
was received with a sullen "Who the devil are
you?" and on explaining his business, Sir Thomas
rejoined, "Then I hope you are not such a damned

---

* Leigh Hunt's Journal, No. 6, for Jan. 11, 1851.

scoundrel as your predecessor." Sir Thomas seems to have been in the habit of dealing out abuse the most flagrant towards those with whom he was brought into contact. "On one occasion,"—we may follow Sir Charles Napier's words,—"the senate having been assembled in the saloon of the palace waiting in all form for his Excellency's appearance, the door slowly opened and Sir Thomas walked in with the following articles of clothing upon him :

"One shirt, which like Tam o' Shanter's friend, the cutty-sark,

"In longitude was sorely scanty."

"One red night-cap,

"One pair of slippers.

"The rest of his Excellency's person was perfectly divested of garments. In this state he walked into the middle of the saloon, looked round at the assembled senators and then said, addressing the secretary, "Damn them, tell them all to go to hell."*

What reception this outburst provoked from the assembled notables we are not informed. When Thurlow once at a dinner-party administered a simi-lar admonition to a blundering man-servant, telling him

* 'The Colonies,' by Col. C. J. Napier, 1833.

he wished he was in hell, the terrified man wearily replied, " I wish I was, my lord ! I wish I was." There can be little doubt that the practice of gentlemen " damning themselves as black as butter-milk " was intended to overawe, and on the whole it has answered the intention. It is however but a cheap substitute for authority, and belongs of right to a rampant jingoism of a past age. We are here reminded of a kind of oath which, having conferred a nick-name upon a political party, seems likely to pass into the language in some altered form. The " Jingos," as will be remembered, were the faction in the country who favoured an aggressive policy during the recent Russian war. The name came to be given them from a circumstance of quite an insignificant kind. At a certain London singing-room a patriotic song happened to be nightly delivered, in which the vocalist emphasised his warlike utterances with a constant recurrence of this oath. The Radicals seized the moment, and in a short space of time the term " by Jingo " was pinned to the backs of the Tory party like a tin kettle tied to a dog's tail. Men soon began to ask themselves where first they could have met with this undignified expression ? The 'Ingoldsby Legends' seemed the most likely ground, only that readers of Goldsmith referred to the example of

the town-bred lady who, when introduced into the
Vicar's family, swore "by the living Jingo!"

Moreover, the term is to be observed in the earliest
translation of Don Quixote (III. vi.): "by the living
jingo, I did but jest," and in Rabelais (v. xxviii.): "by
jingo, I believe he would make three bites of a cherry."
To seek for the origin of the oath, we should have to
turn to a somewhat singular source.   We should find
it as far away as the slopes of the Pyrenees, where
Basque peasants have long sworn by *Jincoa*, that in
fact being the Basque name for God.

We have made mention of Swift in a way that might
favour the presumption that his ridicule was not at
any time directed against the subject of oath-taking.
That such is hardly the case will be seen from his prospectus of the Bank of Swearing, where this overgrown
distempered plant is singled out as a fair butt for his
sallies.   The nature of the business proposed to be
transacted at this fanciful banking-house may be more
aptly considered in another chapter.

CHAPTER VII.

" *Viola.* Swear as if you came but new from the knighting.
Fust. Nay; I'll swear after £400 a year."
Decker's Honest W.

WRITTEN during the fever of South Sea speculation,
the skit of Jonathan Swift, known as the "Bank of
Swearing," was one exceedingly felicitous and well-
timed. We are amused even now, as we read the
prospectus of this preposterous undertaking, at the
extreme audacity with which the would-be projector
solemnly enumerates its advantages. Impossible and
altogether ludicrous as was the enterprise, it is not
improbable that many of the eager financiers of that
speculative age fancied they saw solid reason in the
scheme. It is only to be hoped that they did not too
eagerly respond to the facilities for investment which
the Swearers' Bank was reputed to hold out.

The notion was simply that of a chartered bank
established upon a novel basis and financing upon an
original principle. Such bank was in fact to enjoy a
monopoly of levying the fines which the laws of the

country imposed upon swearing. Although these penalties had been rarely inflicted, the mere circumstance of their being warranted by the statute-book was regarded by the projector in the light of a mine of latent wealth. A profitable banking concern once fairly in operation, and backed by the security of these statutory imposts, what more could the investor require for his capital?

To convince the investing public of the merits of his scheme, he proceeds to calculate the sums that might be realised by fully putting the act into vigour. The neglected statute upon the basis of which the whole of this superstructure was to be raised and the Bank of Swearing endowed, was the act of the sixth and seventh year of William and Mary, inflicting a penalty at the rate of not less than a shilling an oath.*

"It is computed by geographers,"—so argues the promoter—" that there are two millions in the kingdom [Ireland], of which number there may be said to be a

---

* If any person or persons shall . . . . profanely swear or curse . . . . for every such offence the party so offending shall forfeit and pay to the use of the poor of the parish where such offence or offences shall be committed the respective sums hereinafter mentioned; that is to say, every servant, day-labourer, common soldier, or common seaman, one shilling; and every other person two shillings; and in case any of the persons aforesaid shall, after conviction, offend a second time, such person shall forfeit and pay double, and if a third time treble the sum respectively.—6 & 7 *William and Mary*, c. 11.

million of swearing souls. It is thought there may be
five thousand gentlemen. Every gentleman, taken one
with another, may afford to swear an oath every day,
which will yearly produce one million eight hundred
and twenty-five thousand oaths; which number of
shillings makes the yearly sum of £91,250.

" The farmers of this kingdom, who are computed to
be ten thousand, are able to spend yearly five hundred
thousand oaths, which gives £25,000 ; and it is conjectured that from the bulk of the people twenty or five
and twenty thousand pounds may be yearly collected."

The swearing capacity of the army is no less
minutely investigated. In the case of the militia,
however, the promoter is disposed to recommend either
a partial immunity from the tax or else a scale of fines
considerably cheapened. To put the law in full force
against militiamen, at least so opines the promoter,
would only be to fill the stocks with porters and the
pawnshops with accoutrements. So essential is this
point with him, that he makes direct appeal to his
Protestant countrymen, reminding them of the satisfaction it would afford the Papists to see a most useful
body of soldiery actually swear themselves out of their
swords and muskets.

Inclined to a politic leniency towards the military

I

classes, it would seem that this ingenious projector
looked mainly for his revenue to the swearing dues that
might be collected at wakes and fairings. The oaths
of a single Connaught fair, he has calculated, amount
to upwards of three thousand. " It is true," he allows,
" that it would be impossible to turn all of them into
money, for a shilling is so great a duty on swearing,
that if it were carefully exacted, the common people
might as well pretend to drink wine as to swear, and an
oath would be as rare among them as a clean shirt."
In this way the Reverend Dean rattles on. He is
pointing his satire both at the epidemic of financial
adventure then so fatally prevalent and at that incomprehensible leaning to the use of "bad language" of
which even he was so ready to avail himself when it
either suited his purpose or strengthened his style.

The Dean can scarcely be supposed to have known
that one of the many proposals put before Lord
Burghley in the very early days of political economy,
bore a close resemblance to his manner of handling
oaths. A Monsieur Rodenberg proposed to show how
the revenue could be increased to twenty millions of
crowns, and part of his plan consisted in a rigorous
levy of fines on swearing. He further recommended
that a council of twelve "grave persons" should have

the disposal of the fund, which while unexpended should be put out to usury.*

A recommendation of this kind urged upon Queen Elizabeth's ministers was very much in advance of English politics. It so far denotes a turning-point in the history of swearing, that we cannot do better than trace out what the future course of legislation was to be.

Previous to the period we are now entering, a person addicted to intemperate language might have been called to account by his church, or at the bar of his own conscience. He could not have been called to account by the State. The suggestion of State interference, so far as concerns the southern division of this island, seems not to have previously occurred, and we are consequently justified in inferring that the necessity for it had never seriously arisen. There is, indeed, complete cohesion and consistency in what was happening. We believe we have shown elsewhere whence it was, and when it was, that the English people first began to swear, and we are confirmed in our conclusions by finding that this was the precise period at which English law-makers began to legislate upon swearing.

Passing over barbarous and obsolete laws of a more

---

* Coll. of State Papers, Domestic, 1595, p. 12.

imperfect civilisation, we find that the first essays in
State control commenced in Scotland. A full half
century before the question came before Elizabeth's
parliament, the sister kingdom had the benefit of a
statute inflicting a monetary penalty upon the use of
oaths. This enactment, passed by the Scottish parliament of 1551, calls for notice upon other grounds
besides those of morality. If a legal document can be
said to partake of a poetic character, it was certainly the
case with this ordinance of Queen Mary, which seems to
have been directly inspired by the metrical labours of
William Dunbar, then lately the national poet.

The verses of Dunbar to which this result can be
partially attributed are those known as 'The Sweirers
and the Devill.' It is certainly remarkable that the
framers of the Act would seem to have prepared its
clauses with Dunbar's poetry open before them. At
all events, the statute literally recites the "ugsome
oaths" that are used by the old versifier. There is a
severity in the statute at which Dunbar himself would
have been surprised had he lived down to Mary's reign.
In particular, it enacts that "a prelate of kirk, earl or
lord," shall for the first offence be fined to the extent of
twelve pennies, but for the fourth the delinquent shall
be banished or imprisoned for a year.

Dunbar's treatment of his subject is very similar to that of the nameless author of the 'Moralité des Blasphémateurs' which we have previously noticed. He supposes the devil to have assumed human shape, an assumption which in those times would have been thought nothing out of the way, and in that guise to be conversing with the traders in a Lowland market. As is usual in these episodes, he invites them to join him in the use of the most delectable oaths that he can lay before them. The honest market-folk are so taken by his allurements that we have the maltman, the goldsmith, the "sowter," and the "fleshor" vieing with one another in their choice of ribaldry. In this friendly contest, needless to say, it is the parish priest who carries off the prize. One hopes that his excuse was as valid as that of the monk in Rabelais. "How now," exclaims Ponocrates, "you swear, Friar John!" "It is only," replies the friar, "to grace and adorn my speech; it is the colour of a Ciceronian rhetoric."

The place in literature left vacant by Dunbar was soon occupied by Lindsay, the

"Sir David Lindsay of the Mount
Lord Lion, king at arms,"

whose name and titles are so familiar to the readers of Scott. He likewise appears to have led up to the

impending legislation, if not indeed to have leen the
immediate cause of it.   His 'Satyre of the Three
Estaitis,' performed at Coupar in 1535, besides containing other objectionable matter, is a wild medley of
oaths.

Apart from what was passing in and near the
capital, the local authorities from Glasgow to Aberdeen
were up in arms against swearers before any movement
of the kind had taken place in the other division of the
island.   To judge from the borough records of the
former city,* the prevalency of the habit was a source
of great scandal to the presbytery of that town.   The
number of Janet Andersons and William Crawfords
who were arraigned before the high bailiff for offences
of this character is something considerable.   At Aber-
deen† in 1592 the attention of the council was specially
engaged in repressing the swearing of "horrible and
execrable oaths."   They proceeded to put on foot a
system of fines, and with a degree of confidence that is
hardly commendable, they authorised the heads of
families to keep a box in which to place the mulcts
they were empowered to inflict in their households.
Servants' wages were liable to be taxed at the will of

---

* Borough records of the City of Glasgow, 1573–1581.
† Aberdeen Presbytery Records, printed by the Spalding Club.

their masters, and wives' pin-money at the instance of their lords. A few years later the presbytery went further than even the magistracy had already done. They directed the master of the house to keep a "palmer," or instrument for inflicting pain upon the palm of the open hand. This we suppose to have been the last argument used against offenders whose wages or whose pin-money had been sworn away. Altogether the attempt to make people moral by Act of Parliament seems to have been productive of much strife in Scotland, without securing, so far as can be perceived, any positive gain. The Act of 1551, that under which the local and spiritual authorities derived their powers, was further supplemented by Acts of 1567 and 1581.

We now arrive at the point at which legislation upon the subject was to cross the border and take a prominent place in the counsels of King James' reign.

We have seen that it was Queen Elizabeth's godson Sir John Harington, who first recorded the positive introduction of the damnatory oath. A long time, however, must have elapsed before the bantling took heart of grace and found strength to run alone. An examination of Elizabethan writings does not conduce to the idea of the term having had a widespread acceptation.

The reference we have given to the comedy of Nat Field, 'Amends for Ladies,' tends to show that the British shibboleth was still regarded as of exotic growth. The truth would seem to be that the literature of the country, gross and abusive as it often was, was singularly free from terms of this particular description, while the conversation of the humbler orders was not so unexceptionable. Already it had become a source of uneasiness to the Legislature. In 1601 a measure was introduced into the Commons "against usual and common swearing," but, having been carried up to the Lords, it dropped after the first reading. This would appear to have been the first attempt at legislation on the subject.* On the accession of James I. the topic was again brought to the notice of the House, but the early Parliaments of this reign were too much occupied with the work thrown upon them in

---

* Within the precincts of royal palaces regulations seem to have been made from time to time to clear the atmosphere of all impious particles. According to a work by Alexander Howell, the Dean of St. Paul's, printed in 1611, King Henry I. prescribed a scale of fines according to a table as follows :—

"If he were
- a Duke 40 shillings.
- a Lord 20 do.
- a Squire 10 do.
- a Yeoman 3s. 4d.
- a Page, to be whipt."

'*A Sword against Swearers*,' 1611.

consequence of the Gunpowder Treason to formulate any code for the regulation of this abuse. Although no less than five separate bills, having the prevention of swearing for their object, were presented during the course of this reign, it was not until 1623 that an enactment was finally carried defining and controlling the offence. The statute of that year * provided that every offender should forfeit the sum of twelve pence. In default of payment the culprit was to be placed in the stocks for three hours, or if under the age of twelve years was to be severely whipped.

The attack made by the Puritans upon performances of a dramatic nature had resulted in a kindred piece of legislation especially affecting the stage. By an Act † passed in 1606 it was provided that a penalty of 10_l._ should be borne by every person who jestingly or profanely used the name "of God, or of Christ Jesus, or the Holy Ghost, or of the Trinity," in any interlude, pageant or stage-play. It was in consequence of the rigour of this enactment that Ben Jonson narrowly escaped a prosecution for blasphemy. On the production of the 'Magnetic Lady,' the language employed upon the stage gave great offence in legal quarters, and the author was sent for from a sick-bed and severely

* 21 Jac. I. c. 20.   † 3 Jac. I. c. 21.

questioned by the Master of the Revels. An examination of the play will show the charge, as against Jonson, to have been unfounded; even the author was at a loss to understand the occasion for the accusation being preferred. The actors in the piece were accordingly called together, and when confronted with the dramatist, were forced to admit that the objectionable expletives were those of their own supplying.

When some months later the play of 'The Wits' was presented to the licenser, previous to its production on the stage of the Blackfriars, that dignitary was particularly careful to expunge all such passages as struck him as unparliamentary. Sir William D'Avenant, the author of the comedy, complained to the king of this exercise of the censorship, and His Majesty, after reading the play for himself, negatived the decision of the licenser. He ruled that the words "s'death," "s'light," and such kindred terms, were asseverations merely, and not oaths. The court functionary does not appear to have been any the more satisfied, and has left an entry in his diary, submitting indeed to his master's judgment, but maintaining his own opinion. The play was returned to D'Avenant, having the full sanction of the king, who on its first production took boat to the Blackfriars playhouse to witness the performance.*

The stage has continued to enjoy a species of traditional immunity from all the reprobation which swearing is presumed to incur. So long as the action passing on the boards is in ever so remote a degree in affinity with its supposed natural counterpart, and is suited with dialogue that is fairly appropriate, the use of expletives is not omitted in deference to the susceptibilities of an audience. The theatre may in some sense be called a school of swearing, and in that capacity has frequently brought upon itself the castigations of its appointed supervisors. Of all the censors who from time to time have made a stand against this traditional licence, George Colman is to be remembered as the most violent and the most inconsistent.

As a writer he had scandalised a whole generation of playgoers. The 'Heir-at-Law' and the 'Poor Gentleman,' comedies with which he has permanently benefited stage literature, do not certainly halt at any extreme. His very appointment as censor was due to the bottle-acquaintance that had sprung up with the regent Prince of Wales. Yet so squeamish did he

---

* Office-book of Sir Henry Herbert. Collier's 'History of Dramatic Poetry,' ii. 58.

become when once the official mantle had descended
upon his shoulders, that even the exclamations "lud!"
and "la!" were ruthlessly expunged from productions
submitted to his censorship. The words "Oh, Pro-
vidence!" were also rigidly excised, and the very
names of heaven and hell were flatly condemned as
savouring of irreverence.

Says Mr. Dutton Cook, in treating of this feature of
the Georgian drama:—"Men swore in those days not
meaning much harm or particularly conscious of what
they were doing, but as a matter of bad habit, in
pursuance of a custom certainly odious enough, but
which they had not originated and could hardly be
expected immediately to overcome. In this way
malediction formed part of the manners of the time.
How could these be depicted upon the stage in the
face of Mr. Colman's new ordinance? There was
great consternation among actors and authors. Critics
amused themselves by searching through Colman's own
dramatic writings and cataloguing the bad language
they contained. The list was very formidable. There
were comminations and anathemas in almost every
scene. The matter was pointed out to him, but he
treated it with indifference. He was a writer of plays
then, but now he was Examiner of Plays."

The persecution under which Jonson suffered was due to the steady growth of Puritan principles. Measures of austerity were speedily generated by this ascetic philosophy; and among others we find that a scheme for bringing oaths, in a liquidated shape, to the aid of the national resources, was put into operation. Letters patent were granted in the month of July 1635, for establishing a public department for enforcing the laws against swearing. One Robert Lesley was appointed to the office of chief inquisitor, and was authorised to take all necessary steps for carrying out the act in every parish of the kingdom. Whatever moneys might be realised were to be paid over to the bishops for the benefit of the deserving poor. Lesley appointed deputies in the parishes, who, we notice, were at liberty to deduct 2s. 6d. in the £ for their pains. A copy of one of these appointments to a London parish appears among the State papers, but no balance-sheet from which we might learn something of the " turn-over " of the office appears to be forthcoming.*

With what feelings the army of the Parliament regarded this offence may be gathered from two sentences passed upon offenders convicted under military law. In March 1649, a quartermaster named

* Coll. of State Papers, Domestic, 1635–6.

Boutholmey was tried by council of war for uttering impious expressions. The man was found guilty and condemned to have his tongue bored with a red-hot iron, his sword broken over his head, and himself ignominiously dismissed the service. In the following year a dragoon was similarly sentenced by court-martial to be branded on the tongue.* Even in districts removed from martial severity the monetary tax on oath-taking was frequently demanded. We perceive from a recent writer,† who has collected the ancient records of quarter sessions, that swearing was severely visited upon the lieges of Somerset and Devon. John Huishe, of Cheriton, was convicted for swearing twenty-two oaths. Humfrey Trevitt, for swearing ten oaths, was adjudged to pay 33s. 4d. for the use of the poor. William Harding, of Chittlehampton, was held to be within the act of swearing for saying "Upon my life," and Thomas Buttand was fined for exclaiming "On my troth!"

To glance at Scotland at this time, we find the governing body enacting laws of a more searching and stringent character than any that had preceded them.

* Whitelock's Memorials.

† Quarter Sessions from Queen Elizabeth to Queen Anne, by A. H. A. Hamilton. 1878.

The Parliament of 1645 ordered that whoever should curse or blaspheme should upon a second conviction be "censurable" in the manner prescribed, that is, a nobleman should pay twenty pounds Scots, a baron twenty marks, a gentleman ten marks. The Act anticipates the case of a minister of religion coming under its provisions. The punishment in that case was the forfeit of the first part of his year's stipend. In 1649 a further enactment was passed, the previous one being admittedly too lenient, and in the same session the offence of cursing a parent was made punishable by sentence of death. It is certainly curious to witness the extremes to which the Scottish nation were prepared to go in legislating against the commission of this offence. In 1650, when the country was rushing to arms to resist the invasion of Cromwell, an Act of Parliament was prepared which disqualified for command all officers who were addicted to swearing.

The code which, in this country, had proved sufficient for the Puritans remained in force until the manners of the Restoration had rendered further legislation imperative. This took the shape of the statute of William and Mary, by which, as we have seen, the Dean of St. Patrick's was so greatly exhilarated. After an interval of some fifty years the interference of Parliament was again felt to be necessary, and an Act of George II. was passed which still regulates the law upon the subject of swearing.*

The preamble admits that the existing laws were not sufficiently powerful to meet the circumstances for which they were designed. A more onerous scale of penalties was to be prescribed, commencing with a fine of one shilling in the case of a labourer, and rising to five shillings in the case of a swearer of gentleman's degree. That this measure should not want for publicity, it was ordered to be read quarterly in every church and chapel throughout the kingdom.

A curious instance of punishment for neglect of this saving provision, is noticed in the 'Gentleman's Magazine' for 1772. In July of that year a rich vicar and a poor curate were condemned to pay into the hands of the proper officer a sum of 15l. for neglecting to read in church the Act against swearing. This clause was only repealed by an enactment of the present century.

We have some means of knowing whether the fines recoverable under this statute were in point of fact actually inflicted, and from the importance attached by

* 19 Geo. II. cap. 21. There is also a penalty of 40s. for using profane language in the streets under the Town Police Clauses Act, 1847, and the Metropolitan Police Act, 1839.

the public prints to the decisions of magistrates on this head, we are justified in thinking that the statute was very rarely put into requisition. In the ' Gentleman's Magazine' for July 1751 we read that a woman convicted of uttering a profane oath and unable to defray the shilling penalty, was sentenced to ten days' hard labour in Bridewell. In December of the same year a tradesman was committed for a matter of three hundred and ninety oaths, the fines amounting to upwards of 20l., which he was unable to pay. Convictions under the statute were at this time seriously attracting public attention. That the calculations of Dean Swift should not be altogether lost to the world, one rigid economist practically entertained the notion of adding to the national resources by preaching a crusade against the opulent classes of swearers. There was a Mr. Matthew Towgood, who in 1746 prepared a treatise ' Upon the Prophane and Absurd use of the Monosyllable Damn.' It is enough to say that neither imagination nor research seem to have been the especial gift of Mr. Towgood. It is a whining piece of work, in which the author gravely informs us that he had taken up his residence at a seaport town in order the more closely to observe the impious language of the sailors. We should, however, do the author the justice to refer to the one distinctive

K

experience he seems to have gathered in his marine retreat. He had discovered,—so at least he solemnly assures us,—that the monosyllable in question was a "hortatory expression" by which the chaplains in His Majesty's navy were accustomed to summon British seamen to their prayers.

But much as it enters into the penal administration of the seventeenth century, there is little to indicate that the vice was countenanced in high places, or that it was seriously regarded as a pardonable incident pertaining to the enjoyments of men of rank. That crowning distinction seems to have been reserved for the age of Anne and the first sovereigns of the house of Brunswick. Then it was that the insular propensity grew impudent and headstrong, and soon became a power in the land. It is only probable that the moral relapse that followed the Restoration may have given the first impetus to the ascendancy of this invigorating habit. Charles II. is said to have taught his ladies to swear like parrots, but oaths were still only the plaything and not part of the serious business of the Court. The Foppingtons and Clumsys were scrupulously nice in their methods of affirmation, but it was publicly recognised that their swearing was a mere theatrical device, and that they either swore like cavaliers or swore like chambermaids. The acme had not even then been reached. That point was only attained in the age when Duchess Marlborough found disguise impossible by reason of her oaths. In the matter of swearing the courtiers of the Stuarts may have demeaned themselves like Mantalinis, but the giants of a later day swore home. An obscure American clergyman, having undertaken a voyage across the Atlantic to solicit alms for a pious foundation in Virginia, and urging that the people of that state had souls to be saved as well as their brethren in England, was met with the rejoinder from King William's attorney-general, "Souls! damn your souls! make tobacco!"

In the year 1700 there was founded the Society for the Reformation of Manners. It had for one of its prime objects the entire suppression of oath-taking. The society seems to have enrolled members distinguished alike for a laxity of their own morals and a tender solicitude for the welfare of other people's. The King Consort, "Est-il-possible," was persuaded to become a fellow, and was induced to put forth a howling manifesto upon the iniquities of the age. This exordium was publicly read at Bow Church. What with openly declaiming against the hideousness of vice and proceeding criminally against its professors, the society convinced the diarist Evelyn that they were working a complete reformation in the habits of the community.

The building of Saint Paul's Cathedral was proceeding at this time, and the work necessarily employed a large body of labourers and workmen, who, as things were and are, were not scrupulously delicate in the choice of words. Nevertheless, it was the particular care of the builders that not one offensive word should be used during the progress of the work.* Sir Christopher Wren framed rules which made a delinquency in this respect liable to be so summarily visited that it has been the boast of many earnest and slightly credulous people that the mighty fabric was piled up without an oath being spoken. The society certainly did good work if they had any hand in this result.

In spite of the society, the question of swearing and its prevalent grossness seems to have attracted the attention of the civil courts of law at this time. In a number of Applebee's Journal for 1723, some account is given of a certain Abel Boyer, an infamous scribbler and notorious swearer of the day. It seems he had threatened some of his fellow journalists with the

* J. P. Malcolm, 'Manners of London during XVII. Century.'

pains of libel because they had done him simple justice
in referring to the comminations he was accustomed to
use in speech.   Before commencing his suit, Abel pru-
dently sought the advice of counsel, contending that
his trifling derelictions did not partake of the colour of
blasphemy.   The lawyers accordingly gave it against
Mr. Boyer, advising that his "goddams" and kindred
expletives came entirely within the prohibited pale.
In March 1718, there is another instance of swearing
being food for Westminster Hall, as appears from the
Flying Post, the prominent Whig journal of the day.
Mr. Richard Burridge, a scurrilous newsman attached
to the *British Gazetteer*, had been tried at Hicks's Hall
for addiction to blasphemous expressions, too shocking,
says the *Post*, to be named.   Burridge was very
properly convicted, although a strong presentation was
made in his favour, that when sober a better conducted man did not exist.   To account for this person's
unfortunate relapse, it was urged that he was "exces-
sively drunk," a consideration that so weighed with
the tribunal, that they passed upon him what was admitted on all hands to be a most moderate sentence.
Burridge was ordered to take up a position at the New
Church in the Strand and to be from there publicly
whipped to Charing Cross.   Further, he was to pay a

fine of twenty shillings and be imprisoned for a month.
Thenceforward a paper war was waged between the
two political divisions of journalism.   The Tories professed to see the Whig journalists stigmatised by the
disgrace of one of their number, and the great Daniel
Defoe cast censure upon them and upon Burridge from
Mist's Journal, the Tory paper he conducted.

And so, pursued by judgments of court and branded
with letters of infamy, it would seem to have been a
very desperate time for these unfortunate swearers.
The profession of the pen was likely enough to rankle
under this load of aspersion, were it not that a more
genial influence had arisen that was bent upon
remedying rather than provoking offences.   For while
the leaders of opinion were playing their intensest
game of political intrigue, while poets were occupied
with the trade of admiration, and divines with the
trade of subserviency, there arose in England a gentler
and more captivating literature of reproval, that laid
its generous laws upon men the most intolerant and
the most prurient.   We allude to that more benevolent
code of morality inaugurated by Joseph Addison.

CHAPTER VIII.

" *Lackwit.* Now do I want some two or three good oaths to
express my meaning withall. An they would but learn me to
swear and take tobacco I 'tis all I desire."—' *A fine Companion,*'
by *Shackerley Marmion*, 1633.

THIS one voice of kindly censure was that of a man
incapable of a literary mistake. Whatever his own
personal blunders, it was impossible for Joseph Addison
to err in a point of literary judgment. Although
wedded to the society of men of taste and perception,
it was no part of his purpose to remove himself from
contact with the coarsest of human ware. The tolerance
he exhibited in ordinary intercourse reflects itself in
the labours of his pen. In his philanthropies, as in
his severities or his rebukes, he assumes no tinge of
sanctity, no moralist's sad-coloured robe. He is familiar, and in a manner identified, with the very follies
he is so generously decrying. The society into which
he went was disposed to be exceedingly lenient to
fashionable excesses. And thus it was that in the
fulness of his wisdom, it pleased him to be of good

accord with priest and prelate as with the very movers
and seconders of iniquity.

And so, in the consideration of any social folly of his
time and ours, we are in a moment impelled to ask—
What does Mr. Spectator say to this; or gentle Master
Tatler? Even in the present inquiry there can be no
reasonable doubt of their competency to give us
testimony. Addison may have heard as many and as
furious oaths as any man of his time. His ways were
beset by inveterate and uncontrollable swearers. His
friend Steele had a tongue that was foolish enough,
heaven knows; and when he was wont to meet with
Swift in St. James' Coffee House, may he not too often
have been assailed with language needlessly expressive?
What cronies he must have had! what lads he must
have known! He had seen all the tearing fellows of
the day—the three-bottle men at the October Club, the
young blood of the shires who rode into the gap at
Blenheim. He could have remembered the roughest
livers of King Charles' time, Sedley and Rochester,
Bully Dawson and Fighting Fitzgerald. He was
surrounded with bravado and devilry, with all the
disbanded sins of the Flanders regiments. For these
were the days of Ramilies and Malplaquet, when the
nation was intoxicated with her meed of victory; when

his Grace of Marlborough won the country's battles, and his Lord of Peterborough scattered sovereigns from his chariot to show the people he was *not* the Duke of Marlborough. It was a time of great profusion and great excess, in curses as in everything else.

And so, Joseph Addison, though living in the flighty times you did, there can be no doubt of the quiet evenness of your ways, or how jovial were the companions who shook you by the fist. But how you drilled and moulded them, how you held and swayed them by the force of your bright intelligence, how shall we who never heard your voice be able to determine? Happily in the pages of the 'Tatler' and 'Spectator' there is stored up for us the best and rarest of that quiet wisdom. No matter whether the night were studious or riotous, there arrives the punctual morning sheet with its offering of sober satire and sprightly sense. He goes about his task of persuading and humanising as gaily as a man might set out to laugh at a comedy. He mounts his best ruffles and his finest tunic as he sits down to write his homily.

It is with no halting, staid, discriminative pen that he descants upon the pleasantries and follies, the very reference to which give life and colour to a weary argument. By the aid of these threads of human sentiment we fancy we come the closer to him in his musings and his wanderings, now hieing, as he does, to the pantiles or the playhouse, now to the Temple Stairs or Vauxhall Gardens. Posterity takes delight in reversing the footsteps of its favourites. It attempts to return with them to the scenes which they themselves have left for good so long ago. And so with Addison, we accustom ourselves to see him mixing in a crowd of masquers and dominos, or supping in upper chambers with ministers of state and tavern wits. The fancy is a harmless one, and not far removed from reality. Imagine, therefore, Mr. Joseph Addison at Hockley-in-the-Hole or at Cupar's Gardens, but be sure that to-morrow's sermon will want nothing of its grace and sparkle because inspired over-night in a mug-house parlour.

Addison has in fact conceived and transmitted to us some of the loftiest notions ever formed of a Deity, and of the unending trespass against divine law. Among surroundings possibly resonant with ribaldry, he could reflect, as few before him have so impartially and equally reflected, how much of vileness is to be set down to the score of thoughtlessness and inanity, how much to a high-handed defiance of the Master he owns. One number of the 'Spectator,' that of November 8th,

1711, sends forth the sternest challenge to the government of error. Few other secular works have made so moderate and at once so eloquent a protest. Adapting the notion of Locke that the unaided realisation of the Deity is formed by observation of the qualities we should desire to find in ourselves, but sublimated by the notion of infinity attaching to each of them, Addison proceeds to argue a state of veneration being the normal condition of the mental frame. The horror that is conceived by a child, or, as it may be, by a grown man, at the jarring dissonance of an oath is nothing else than a sense of injury dealt out to this deeply-rooted conviction. A condition of reverence being thus inherent, it follows that the images which reason has unconsciously reared must meet with some disturbing shock before they can be impaired or dismembered. But the blow once fairly delivered, the victim of the assault in too many cases passes out into the ranks of the assailants. The boundary line between the state of abhorrence and the succeeding one of aggression is so faint that it may almost imperceptibly be overpassed, and is apt to become the more obscure with growth of years.

The danger is so easily incurred by even right-thinking men, that Addison enjoins perfect abstinence from the passing mention of the name of the Deity, instancing the Jewish prohibition which forbad its use even in professedly religious discourses. And in this point of veneration, we shall find the practice of Judæa to have been more precise than anything that is recorded of a nation. Apart from the high deliberative swearing that was so severely visited by the Mosaic law, the use of most unmeaning and flippant particles was met with signal retribution. The man who standing in the Syrian market-place made mention of the holy name in reference to the common incidents of the day—to the lusciousness of the melons, the knavery of the merchants—a mere impatient whisper, perhaps, in all the hubbub of the fair, was instantly deprived of civil rights. He had lost all power of intercourse or conversation. He could not appear at a feast of three or a congregation of ten; he could not mourn for a brother or bury a child. The sentence was only removed after thirty days of expiation.

In the 'Spectator' of May 6th, in the same year, he recounts an experiment supposed to have been successfully practised in a company of hardened swearers. A host is presented as having invited to his table as many of his friends as were conspicuous for their proficiency in swearing. He takes the pre-

caution to station a shorthand writer in a concealed
part of the room. The repast, as may be supposed,
was rendered terrific by the unceasing clatter of oaths,
but as soon as it had ended, the Amphytrion ushered
in the scribe, who proceeded to read aloud the faithful
report he had taken down. The writer, it would seem,
had filled many sheets with this animated conversation,
but this was found to be so interspersed with swearing
redundancies that the whole might have been sum-
marised in a single page. The perusal of the document, we are informed, so far brought conviction to
the minds of the swearers, that they forthwith began
to work with a will to amend their lives and their
vocabulary.

The indignation of our essayist is without doubt
most powerfully aroused at the inadvertent use that
was made of the sacred name. " What can we think,"
he exclaims, " of those who make use of so tremen-
dous a name in the ordinary expressions of their anger,
mirth, and most impertinent passions? of those that
admit it into the most familiar questions and assertions,
ludicrous phrases and works of humour?" And then,
as if recollecting that gentlemanly example was the
one rule to which the squires and politicians at Button's
or the Kitcat would most readily submit, he instances

a person of position, who, during a long life, was never known to omit a gesture of reverence at the mention of the Deity. It is a noticeable point in the gossiping moralist that he always carefully guards himself from passing upon his readers the affront, for such it would have been esteemed, of directing their attention to the qualities of persons in a presumably lesser position than themselves.

On the whole Mr. Spectator has perhaps done wisely in humouring as well as reprobating. The temper of the times required something less ponderous than the invective of the older school of moralists, and this was the very want that a man of Addison's temperament was best able to supply. The confidence reposed in his readers was not misplaced. The banter and the satire of these graceful essays are acknowledged to be reflected in the mended morality of the whole body of subsequent literature.

If we mistake not, there is the same improvement soon to be witnessed in every department, in the national life of the nation as well as the private life of the citizen. In part attributable to the politic sway of the Walpole government, in part to the tincture of politeness and good breeding that these polished pen-men had striven to disseminate, there is, for a time at least, a marked absence of rancour and strife of tongues.

The fires of the Puritan faction had smouldered out; those of the Jacobite frenzy had hardly had time to re-kindle. That spirit of minute controversy which had never ceased to divide both court and city since the days of Martin Mar-prelate was at length at rest. In this somewhat remarkable lull we find very little giving or taking of abuse. So far as social records are a guide, there seems even to be a calm in the usual tempest of swearing.

But towards the middle of the eighteenth century comes the relapse. Jacobitism had blazed again. The factions were relit. Controversy wagged its tongue as before. Everywhere are evidences of want and misery, of low sedition and of strong drink. The tipsy Duke of Cumberland is the hero whose graces we are to admire. The 'Guards' march to Finchley' is the picture which may be trusted to convey a portraiture of the manners of the times. It is precisely at this conjuncture that Parliament enacted the last and most stringent of the measures by which it sought to place an embargo upon swearing. In the use of coarse and violent language women competed with the men. In 1756 on the occasion of the memorable trial concerning

the fair fame of the Countess of Grosvenor, the letters
of this lady were produced and read in court.   We
have Horace Walpole's authority for saying that the
oaths with which they were plentifully besprinkled
were far more masculine than they can be said to have
been tender.   The prince of the blood to whom they
were addressed could swear volubly too, and his oaths
we may feel assured were neither masculine nor tender.

We of this generation can scarcely have any adequate notion of what the swearing has been which has
prevailed in this country at different periods, and more
particularly in the latter part of the reign of George II.
So popular and so ungovernable was the habit, that
there is hardly any rational means to be found for
accounting for it.   At this time there lived in an
obscure village in Sussex a decent, well-to-do tradesman, whose shop, well stocked with broadcloth and
homespun, was a centre of commerce for miles around.
He was known to be a thriving man, and seems to
have taken a leading part in the administration of
parish affairs.   Business was not so burdensome
but that he found time to attend at every festive
gathering, and to keep a well-written chronicle of his
own and his neighbours' doings.   This diary has of
late years been unearthed, and a very pretty story it

has to tell of the *bourgeois* manner of life towards the meridian of the century.* One entry will speak for many of the same character.

"February 5th, 1759.—In the evening I went down to the vestry; there was no business of moment to transact, but oaths and imprecations seemed to resound from all sides of the room. I believe if the penalty were paid assigned by the legislature by every person that swears that constitute our vestry, there would be no need to levy any tax to maintain our poor."

The outbreak must have reached an unprecedented point when we find the president of quarter sessions, Sir John Fielding, alluding to it in the charge to the grand jury delivered at the Guildhall in April, 1763. No language can be stronger than that of Sir John— "I cannot sufficiently lament," he says "that shameful, inexcusable and almost universal practice of profane swearing in our streets; a crime so easy to be punished, and so seldom done, that mankind almost forget it to be an offence, and to our dishonour be it spoken, it is almost peculiar to the English nation."

A state of things like this would seem to have given

* "Diary of a Sussex Tradesman a hundred years ago," printed in Sussex Arch. Coll., vol. xi.

L

rise to a singular communication addressed to the
'Gentleman's Magazine.' The writer lays the whole
blame upon the clergy; they have offered a direct
encouragement to swearing by declaring it a sin. He
recommends that divines in future should describe it
as a virtue, which, he says, may be as easily done as
saying the contrary, and he will answer for the success
of the experiment. A clergyman of his acquaintance,
continues the writer, had already carried this bit of
precept into use. To convince the congregation that
swearing was far from being a sin, this gentleman
constantly practised it in his own discourses. There
might indeed be some doubt here which was the worse,
the remedy or the disease.

The imprecations that are so severely censured by
Fielding are a totally different thing from the imprecations patronised by Lady Grosvenor, if we are
to understand the oaths of the populace to have been
the hideous and unsightly objects presented for condemnation to the Middlesex jury. And here we hardly
need point out the distinction between swearing when
at its earnest, and swearing when at its play. In
numberless courts and alleys, in the sinks and hiding-
places of a great city, we may be sure there are innumerable spots where oaths and imprecations never for

a moment are laid aside. They are as punctual and as regular as the ticking of a clock. No word is uttered that has not its accompaniment of an oath ; no bread broken that is not devoured with cursing. For why? Human nature is at all times bent upon possessing, and upon increasing what it has acquired. The very act of producing is sufficient to uphold the equilibrium of the mental frame. But this same nature, when pinched and starved, becomes a perfect storehouse of enmity and ill-feeling. Among the denizens of these holes and crannies humanity has been driven very hard. It has been crushed and bruised to a point beyond endurance. The possibility of possessing is very faint, that of enjoying still more remote. No graceful thing—no pleasant thing, can readily come to its hand. Yet there is one chattel they *can* possess when every stick and stone is denied them. They can be tenacious of their swearing. See how manifestly useful a thing it is! It can give a man an eloquence where none would otherwise belong to him. It can set him up with a semblance of bodily strength, when otherwise he would be puny and fragile. He can assail authorities, and they dare not answer. He can drown down the voice of missionaries, and they are halting in reproval. There are beings so dejected—so

L 2

penurious—that this swearing constitutes their whole
store of worldly opulence. They know it too, in a
fashion, although it has never been told them and they
themselves are incapable of the telling.

So much for swearing when in grim earnest; how
are we to account for it in its transition to sport and
play? Unless we are greatly mistaken, there has
entered into its composition a spirit of broad humour
which has, in a manner, rendered it attractive, if not
positively amusing. Were we to put the whole body
of bad language to a judicial trial, we should in fairness
be compelled to admit the extenuating circumstance of
a time-expired claim to the mock-heroic and the ludicrous. It certainly does not sparkle now, but it must
have come of a witty stock, and have boasted a mirth-
próvoking pedigree. To have rendered itself so particularly palatable as it has done, like many other
kinds of verbal folly, it can only have taken its rise
in a perverted spirit of merriment.

To apply words, and more especially adjectives, in an
unwonted and unusual sense is one of the arts which
go a long way to make conversation agreeable. To do
this with taste, and without corrupting or annihilating
the meaning of the word, demands a certain amount
of literary skill. To do so at any price frequently

demands skill, and is always fraught with consequences of some kind to the listener. Most of these perversions of highly respectable words have now become so trite that they pass unchallenged. The verb "to bag," for instance, is in jocular use for implying a petty appropriation of property. It must of course at some time have been forcibly wrested from the language of sportsmen, and no doubt with this circumstance secretly underlying it, has been productive, and will be again, of general good-humour. Such another *tour de phrase* is met with in the verb "to charter." This originally had reference to the hiring of a ship; but when we hear of chartering a fly, or chartering a stretcher, there certainly arises an odd sense of the incongruous. We are far from saying that the merriment in these cases is acute, but we contend that this kind of pleasantry is at the bottom of every phrase or catchword obtaining universal acceptance.

Examples might be multiplied of this wanton abduction of words. The not very polite expression "the damage," as signifying the cost of any article of purchase, is one which upon frequent repetition may fail to strike the mind as containing any element of humour. But recollecting the wide region the imagination has to traverse in order to connect the idea of detriment with the idea of price, we are disposed to allow that this mental circuit is enlivened with some shreds of grotesque imagery. Indeed, a large and by no means contemptible portion of the world have derived a high degree of enjoyment from the simple confusion and dislocation of terms. Nothing is more frequent than to find a catch-word ostensibly of no kind of intelligence being exchanged by delighted youths across half the desks and counters of the metropolis. The flippant use of oaths is so far practically explained ; the colloquial habit of imputing to unoffending objects a condition of damnation passing in the light of a fairly respectable joke. Joke indeed there is none, but it is the popular repute or suspicion of a jest that exercises this fascination. It is noticeable that a provincial audience witnessing one of Colman's or Sheridan's comedies is more genuinely amused by the " zounds " and " dammes " uttered in provoking situations by testy speakers, than by all the polish of epigram and dialogue.

As further illustrating this latent element of humour, which has helped to perpetuate the practice of purposeless swearing, we may be permitted to refer to an occurrence that befell us when, some number of years ago, we happened to be taking a humble part in a legal inquiry at a county assizes. The case was one in which, let us say, Moribundus was plaintiff, and the Juggernaut Railway Company were defendants. It is not necessary to refer to the business of the dispute further than to say that the plaintiff had been shattered almost beyond recovery, and that our province it was to help to prove to demonstration the utter untrustworthiness of the story relied upon by Moribundus. The repast that succeeded the inquiry more nearly concerns us; the lawyers, the London doctor, and the local practitioner having agreed thus to celebrate the evening. We do not recollect that the company were at all disposed to fraternity, as a degree of professional acrimony seemed to preside at that feast. In the course of dinner, one of the party, looking round the board, happens to inquire, "Where's the damned mustard?" No particular notice is taken of this remark, until presently one of the legal gentlemen solemnly observes, "Where's the damned salt?" We do not attempt to explain it, but a sudden sense of the ludicrous instantly overcame the men of law and medicine assembled at the *Fleece*. This incongruous and perfectly irrelevant joinder of words, while it revealed the source from which amusement was supposed to flow, was at the same time a potent

satire upon the practice of a disreputable art. It
was taking the name of swearing itself in vain. It
substituted for any closer argument the incisive logic
of ridicule.

It occurs to us to notice that Shakespeare, who
was certainly alive to the hidden springs of swearing,
has conceived the notion of winging much the same
folly with a precisely similar shaft. It had been the
fashion among the gay Ephesians of Eastcheap, during
Elizabeth's reign, to swear by their honour. "Where
learnt you that oath, fool?" asks Rosalind. "Of a
certain knight," returns Touchstone, "who swore by
his honour they were good pancakes."

With these examples of compromise before us, it
becomes almost a matter for regret that there should
remain so large a body of protectionists whose resentment at anything savouring of an oath is perhaps
one of the surest means of perpetuating swearing.
Among the severest codes devised to check the progress
of the vice was that designed by the Puritan settlers in
Connecticut and Rhode Island. These Blue Laws, as
they were called, aimed at establishing an almost
theocratic form of government. Adopting the polity
of Great Britain as a standpoint, these enactments
went considerably further and sought to remodel that

system upon the basis of the severest of Jewish ordinances. Among offences to which the Puritan mind would seem to have been especially averse are to be numbered those of swearing and tobacco-smoking. In the case of the latter, however, retribution was only visited upon the after-generation of smokers. People who had already acquired the habit were free to continue in it for the days of their life. In the case of swearing, needless to say, no such licence was extended, convicted swearers being liable to be dealt with according to the gravity of the offence. The penalty seems to have been rated in some instances as low as a fine of five shillings, and to have amounted in others to the punishment of death.

In all countries enactments have been levelled against the excesses of ejaculation, but the true instruments for keeping them in bounds, assuming there to be an actual necessity for such treatment, has been shown to be the voice of ridicule and the keen banter of satire. Moralists of the pattern of the law-givers of Connecticut would probably be found to take exception to the oaths of Bobadil, and would condemn ' Every Man in his Humour' as a licentious work. It does not however need argument to show that the mere fact of the redoubted Bobadil taking credit to himself

for his freaks with the fourth commandment, forms one
of the strongest inducements to respect that prohibition.
But in view of any latent admiration being lurking in
any portion of his auditory, Jonson has contrived a
foil in the person of Master Stephen. This is a vain-
glorious, empty parasite, whose clumsy imitation of
the Captain is certainly calculated to put his hearers
out of all sympathy with his model. So captivated is
this apt disciple with Bobadil's string of expletives, that
he is found anxiously inquiring whether he also may
swear *en militaire.* "Certainly," says the sagacious
Well-bred, " if, as I remember, your name is entered in
the Artillery Garden."

Bobadil "swore the legiblest of any man christened."
The field, however, has not been suffered to be left
without competitors. To see how persistent has been
the struggle for reputation in the matter as well as
manner of swearing, we have only to turn to the well-
known dialogue in Sheridan's comedy:

" *Absolute.* But pray, Bob, I observe you have got an
odd kind of a new method of swearing.

" *Acres.* Ha! ha! you've taken notice of it—'tis
genteel, isn't it? I didn't invent it myself though, but
a commander in our militia, a great scholar I assure
you, says that there is no meaning in the common

oaths, and that nothing but their antiquity makes them respectable ; because, he says, the ancients would never stick to an oath or two, but would say, By Jove ! or by Bacchus !—by Mars ! or by Pallas ! according to the sentiment, so that to swear with propriety, says my little major, the oath should be an echo of the sense ; and this we call the oath referential, or sentimental swearing—ha ! ha ! 'tis genteel, isn't it ?

"*Absolute.* Very genteel, and very new, indeed !—and I daresay will supplant all other figures of imprecation.

"*Acres.* Ay, ay, the best terms will grow obsolete. Damns have had their day." *

We are not aware whether it has been noticed how closely this passage is foreshadowed by dialogue occurring in a much earlier play. Both turn upon the notion of a species of property being acquired in set forms of swearing. The play in question is from the pen of Richard Brome, and is further useful to our purpose as showing that this eccentricity had not abated in the interval that elapsed between Jonson and Sheridan. Under the title of 'Covent Garden Weeded,' it exposes the riotous doings that prevailed in that joyous locality. It was to cleanse this new plan-

* ' The Rivals,' act ii. sc. 1.

tation of the human nettles and creepers that found
shelter in its precincts that the drama purports to
have been designed. The builders had just completed
the spacious piazza which occupies a portion of the site
of the convent garden formerly existing there. Among
the rollicking societies that were springing up in this
new settlement, was one known, at least in the comedy,
as the "Brothers of the Blade and the Batoon." One
scene in this play discloses the brethren in a state of
carnival. They are engaged in passing a novice into
the ranks of the order, their captain thus exhorting
the new-comer as to their social code :—

"*Captain.* I have given you all the rudiments and
my most fatherly advice withall.

"*Clot.* And the last is that I should not swear ; how
make you that good ?

"*Captain.* That's most unnecessary, for look you, the
best, and even the lewdest of my sons do forbear it, not
out of conscience, but for very good ends, and instead
of an oath, furnish the mouth with some affected
protestation. *As I am honest!* it is so. *I am no
honest man!* if it be not. *'Ud take me!* if I lie to you.
Nev'rigo! nev'rstir! I vow! and such like.

"*Clot.* I'll have *I vow*, then.

"*Nick.* Nay, but you shall not, that's mine.

"*Clot.* Can't you lend it me now and then, brother?"

It would almost seem, from the evidence of the several passages we have had occasion to refer to, as if the various diversities of character and occupation had engendered a spirit of competition in the assumption of oaths. Whether scholar or soldier, knight or citizen, each man, according to his degree, is burning to distinguish himself by some distinctive and eccentric form of swearing. The asseverations employed by the Shallows and Slenders are as limpid and as timorous as those of Falstaff and Bardolph are downright and headstrong. Hotspur, as we have seen, reproaches Lady Percy for swearing like a comfit-maker's wife. With the rest of the Percies he had lived in Aldersgate Street, and had probably contracted an aversion to everything savouring of the vulgar life of a great city. How defiant and versatile were the expletives of the old French nobility, we may learn from the pages of Brantôme. When seeking to convey a flattering portrait of his father, François de Bourdeilles, he does not omit to impress us with the importance of his oaths. Playing backgammon with Pope Jules II., his form of adjuration was *Chardieu bénit!* when he lost, and *Chardon bénit!* when he won.

In Elizabethan England a ridiculous notion prevailed among town society, associating the idea of good breeding with the use, by way of oath, of the word "protest." Such an affirmation was understood to raise the presumption of quality in the person who used it. Says Carlo Buffone, "Ever, when you can, have two or three peculiar oaths to swear by, that no man else swears, and above all protest." Neither is Shakespeare silent upon this fashionable eccentricity. The Nurse in 'Romeo and Juliet' is instantly won over to the side of the Veronese lover the moment he utters "I protest," and no longer harbours a doubt of his principles. We see her desirous of communicating to her mistress this single expression of gentlemanhood without concerning herself about the more weighty portion of Romeo's message. This is, perhaps, almost beneath the dignity of the love-story, but we have to regard it as a relic. We must understand the allusion as a piece of chaff administered to the gallants and templars who sported their fine clothes and broached their oaths and their jests seated upon the very stage where the performers were playing. A passage in a contemporary, entitled 'Sir Giles Goosecap,' affords a key to the especial estimation in which the term then happened to be held :—"There is not the best duke's son in France dares say *I protest* till he be one-and-thirty years old at least, for the inheritance of that word is not to be possessed before."

Not only do we view these allusions as relics, but we may as justly consider them in the light of literary fossils. The aim and intention of the author have become petrified. It is, in fact, only by the help of study and appreciation that the true shape and proportion of the idea can be adequately revealed. But search beneath the crust of this intellectual spoil-bank, and there will be seen those slight, if somewhat corroded indications which disclose the humour and the temper of a forgotten age. These inconsequent oaths and no less incomprehensible bywords, fit only now-a-days to undetermine critics and to baffle commentary, are really the reflection of a tinsel finery that was no doubt borne aloft and bravely carried in its day. The explanation for this is simple. The player, to be well in with his patrons, had to turn the laugh from side to side, to give a thrust here and a buffet there, just as the mood or the opportunity dictated. It is this easy familiarity with audiences which has filled our play-books with such store of meaningless or half-meaningless expressions. Not that their supposed want of meaning is more than co-extensive with their apparent want of purpose. Once re-animated with a design, and that of ever so trivial a character, and their significance stands out in relief. When, as frequently happens in our reading, we encounter oaths of the pattern which Shakespeare ascribes to the youth of Verona, we may feel sure we have·fallen upon some passing home-thrust, some spectral blow, delivered, as it were, among now ghostly antagonists.

Thus we find that in the town life of the more favoured days of Charles I. it was a common affectation to use the words "refuse me," much as the Elizabethan dandies made mention of the word "protest." We see this indicated by several examples of contemporary raillery, and particularly in the play of 'Match at Midnight,' in which the lordlings of the time are described as "those wicked elder brothers, that swear, *refuse them!* and drink nothing but wicked sack."

So at other periods we find other combinations doing yeoman service in this particular; as, for instance, in Killigrew's play 'The Parson's Wedding,' where Careless is explaining his plan for attacking the affections of the fair sex—"I am resolved to put on their own silence, answer forsooth, swear nothing but *God's nigs.*" Except upon the score of banter at prevailing idiotcies, it would be difficult to account for the luxuriant way in which oaths of this description have been provided.

We may not inaptly before closing this chapter travel into another hemisphere and advert to that side of the subject in which the powers of darkness are accustomed to be apostrophised in place of the powers of light. Most of the swearing which we have had to pass in review may be said to have been accumulated at a vast expense to our notions and perceptions regarding the Source of all light. How is it, then, that the full detriment of this system was never taken into account before, and that the obverse of the present practice was not more generally adopted. One might have supposed that the malignant beings who find so facile an entrance into popular imagination would have been the first objects with which to associate so much that is acrimonious. If this could have been seen to, and thoroughly brought about, it is possible that we should never have heard of "swearing" at all, or that it might very well have occupied the same relative position upon the pedestal of virtues as it now does upon the more degraded tallies of vice. However this may be, and of course speculation upon the subject can be nothing more than fanciful, it is the beneficent creations of the universe, and not the malignant ones, that

M

have absorbed the greater part of the energy directed
to the practice of swearing.

In English archaic writings the instances in which
the mention of the Satanic power is thus utilised are
not numerous. We cannot compete with the *diables*
and *diavolos* of another race. Wherever references of
this kind do occur, they as often assume the shape of
some amusing transposition. The sharp edge is at
once taken off the anathema. Thus the soubriquet
"old Harry" or "the Lord Harry" generally understood to refer to Satan, is frequently used as an adjunct
of strong feeling.* But as an imprecation it is of quite
inferior magnitude, and seems almost to imply the existence of a strain of good-fellowship with the Evil One
which it might be exceedingly impolitic to disturb.

But beyond the intuitive feeling that the cognomen
does apply to this individual, there is little to advance
which can clear up the question as to the precise origin
of the term. It is supposed that our popular notion of
the devil is derived from the Roman fauni. The shaggy
coat, the horns and cloven feet, are certainly peculiar
to the classical treatment of this supernatural being.
It is inferred therefore that the idea has been trans-

---

* " By the Lord Harry ! he should have done with Christmas boxes."
Swift, ' *Journal to Stella*.'

mitted to us through the medium of our early moralities and interludes. This course of descent derives colour from the fact that the like paraphernalia are not the subject of opprobrious mention in the Scriptures,* and that hence our notion of the devil must be drawn from pagan rather than biblical influences. It is accordingly suggested that "old Harry," the subject of so much irreverent and irresponsible reference, is no other than "old hairy" of the earliest phases of theatrical representation.

A jocose turn seems also to have been given to that common contraction of the Satanic name of which Mistress Page makes use in the 'Merry Wives' when she exclaims, "I cannot tell what the dickens his name is!" It does not however seem that the expression can be traced earlier than Heywood's 'Edward the Fourth,' of the date 1600, where we meet with the passage: "What the dickens! Is it love that makes you prate to me so fondly?" The word is, however, less of an oath than an exclamation.

Probably few persons who allow themselves the enjoyment of that rather jocular expletive, *the deuce!* are in the least aware of the remote antiquity of this

---

* The cloven foot is an evidence of a clean beast, and horns are attributed, pictorially at least, to Moses.

delectable figure of speech. It is perhaps the most ancient of all the oaths and apologies for oaths that have come down to us, and which after a long and vicissitudinous transit have arrived at last, neither mutilated or dismembered. So old is it that it dates from the very formation of the language, but of so tainted a pedigree that in spite of some six hundred years of regular descent we can scarcely permit it to hold dictionary rank.

But, if the account we have to give of its origin can be credited, its history is singular as being intimately connected with one of the greatest social changes that have taken place in the national life. When we are told that the Norman conquerors imposed their language upon the subject race, we can understand with what difficulty and hesitation the Saxon thanes would attempt to assimilate the foreign tongue. So severe a lesson could only be learned by grasping at such words and phrases as were the more frequently recurring. To say that oaths and imprecations, and in fact all terms of anger and violence, would leave the more durable impression, is only to insist upon what we see daily exemplified in countries where the like process is going on. So it happened with a very favourite Norman exclamation. From the evidence of the earliest metrical romances we gather that *Deus!* was such a term of impatience as was constantly upon the lips of the descendants of the invaders. But no sooner did these more courtly and cultivated entertainments make their way into English vernacular, than we find that even in this latter shape the Norman *deus* is significantly preserved. There it appears among the rugged doggrel, a piece of continental finery stitched into the homely Saxon garb. It had dropped out of the vocabularies of the French romancists and had become the common property of the ordinary provincial poetaster. It had passed in fact from the French to the English tongue, and is claimed to be that very *deuce* with which we are most of us familiar.

Proof of this is afforded by comparison of the old romance of 'Havelok the Dane'* as it exists in its home and in its foreign versions, and both of which are assigned to a period anterior to the fourteenth century. The translator was evidently a man of spirit, who to warm his Lincolnshire readers has added much original incident and local colouring. Nevertheless he carefully retained the Norman *deus*. It was evidently quite at home on the wolds and in the fens of the translator's

---

* Edited by Sir Frederick Madden for the Roxburgh Club, 1828.

country, and only wanted the accent which Grimsby
patrons would not fail to supply, to transform it to the
expression with which we are so well acquainted.

There seems to be one oath of this description which
bids fair to elude all guess-work as to its origin or
meaning. It was formerly a practice in France to
swear *par le diable de Biterne.* When so much exacti-
tude had been employed to emphasise the whereabouts of
this personage, it is only natural to inquire where the
locality referred to might happen to be. We believe,
however, that no satisfactory answer has as yet been
returned. Some light is thrown upon the question by
Francisque Michel who (in his 'Récherches sur les
Etoffes de Soie') has shown that a present of some rare
pailes de Biterne was sent to Alexander by Candace,
one of the queens of Ethiopia. With this single ray of
illumination we must be content.

CHAPTER IX.

"As I was finishing this worke, an oyster-wife tooke exception against me and called me knave."—'*Lamentable Effect of Two Dangerous Comets*,' 1591.

WE trust that we have travelled thus far on our journey without wounding the susceptibilities of any of our readers, and that thus it may continue to the not distant end. In all probability our remarks and illustrations will have been scanned by two totally diverse classes of patrons, those to whom the topics suggested present much that is worthy of attention, and those to whom this little treatise will appear to be written in almost an unknown tongue. All that we can do is to claim the indulgence of these latter. We hope that they at least will acquit us of any intention of blemishing the fair front of human nature, or of darkening any of the windows that administer to its requirements of light and air. In fine, we trust that what has been said, has been spoken fairly and frankly. Not, however, that we pretend that the views we may have advanced have anything but a local application. There is a swearing world, a place in which people habitually swear, but there is also a non-swearing world in which they are partially if not totally unacquainted with observances of swearing. To present a picture of the former to the dwellers in the more opposite locality is to expect approval of a marine painting from those who have never beheld the sea. The reflections therefore that we may have been called upon to make by the way, no less than the numerous instances we have found it as well to refer to, must be taken as pertaining only to those troubled waters that surge around the continent inhabited of swearers.

This careless, indulgent and pleasure-seeking portion of the world have derived even comfort and convenience from a recognition of the best regulated usages of swearing. Reputations for courage and audacity have thus been hourly established by the careful insinuation of hideous expletives. Friendships have been cemented by the force of this common bond of union; strangers set at their ease; the weak and hesitating have been galvanised into action. Judging from a purely worldly standpoint, it would be inconsistent not to admit that society has been under deep obligations to this especial form of wickedness. Swearing has in the main been rendered agreeable and popular in so far that it has been adopted to span over social distances and level social distinctions, to create in fact a code of easy sympathy between otherwise thoroughly unsympathetic men. The worst—and swearers are not necessarily the worst—no less than the best of mankind endeavour to generate some species of that " touch of nature " which we are told makes the whole world kin. We must not therefore be too severe on finding that this very creditable object is sometimes sought to be accomplished by somewhat discreditable means.

As a few of our readers may by this time have harboured a conviction that swearing is in some degree a social necessity, they will be able to give full scope to the views upon this point of the excellent Mr. Shandy.* The only compunction that seems to have been entertained by this gentleman resided in the danger of expending small curses upon totally inadequate occasions. He maintained, indeed, with the utmost Cervantic gravity, that he had the greatest veneration for that student of swearing who, in obvious mistrust of his own extempore powers, composed forms suitable to all degrees of provocation, and kept them framed over his chimney-piece for daily reference.

* 'Tristram Shandy,' vol. iii. ch. 12.

"I never apprehended," puts in Dr. Slop, "that such a thing was ever thought of—much less executed."

"I beg your pardon," replies Mr. Shandy, "I was reading—though not using—one of them to my brother Toby this morning, whilst he poured out the tea."

The work of ingenuity in question turned out to be a decree of excommunication, certainly a very ponderous and damnatory one, compiled by Ernulphus, a learned bishop of Rochester. Mr. Shandy is understood to account for the comprehensiveness of this anathema by assuming it to have been designed as an institute or perfect digest of swearing. He conjectures that upon a decline of vituperation Ernulphus had with great learning collected all the known methods, for fear of their being dispersed and so lost to the world for ever. The worthy Shandy would even go so far as to maintain that there was no kind of oath that was not to be found in Ernulphus. "In short," he would add, "I defy a man to swear out of it."

This piece of quaintness, as we need hardly point out, only goes to the fact that wide as is the range of imprecation, it must always come back to that one monotonous symbol of despisal. The anathema of the good bishop is pitched in many keys and sounds, like the collected utterances of many throats. But even Ernul-

phus can scarcely have foreseen the Rabelaisian refine-
ments that would suggest themselves to the minds of
men as soon as literary demands were made upon the
well-worn supply.

The genius of the French language seems more particularly to lend itself to the fabrication of burlesque
forms and subterfuges. Thus to affirm by *le sacré froc
d'Habacuc*, or by *la double-triple manche de serpe*, are
fair specimens of the ingenuity that has been lavished.
Far less offending have been the ludicrous forms of
asseveration popular in the lower ranks of French
society, and one of which it is sufficient to mention as
occurring in a curious rhyme of the last century,* where
among other things is found characterised the pseudo-
nuptials of a certain abbess and a dignitary of the
Church—

> " Mais, *par la vertu d'un oignon*,
> Ils sont mariés environ,
> Comme l'est l'évêque de Chartres
> Avec l'abbesse de Montmartres."

It is not improbable that a great deal of the aversion
that is associated with the practice of swearing is due to
the custom of those novelists who are in the habit of
screening their oaths behind the most transparent of

* ' Harangue des Habitans de Sarcelles,' 1740.

disguises. To denote an expletive by its initial letter
followed with a dash is really to attract undue attention
to that which the writer acknowledges himself ashamed
of printing. The contrivance serves no useful purpose,
and, if we are not mistaken, the more robust of modern
novelists have eschewed it altogether. Very different
in this respect is the device adopted by Dickens in one
of the most entertaining of his romances. Readers of
'Great Expectations' will remember the description of
Mr. William Barley. This presents us with a picture
of a water-logged old ship's captain, who, as he lay
through the long hours of the day and night upon his
uneasy mattress, never ceased to hold communion with
himself in anything but a strain of piety—"Ahoy! bless
your eyes, here's old Bill Barley! Here's old Bill
Barley on the flat of his back, by the Lord! Lying on
the flat of his back, like a drifting old dead flounder;
here's old Bill Barley, bless your eyes. Ahoy! Bless
you!" Of course the point of this monologue lies in
the fact that the supposed blessings are really substituted by the novelist for desires of a very opposite
description.

There are few pictures we would less willingly omit
from the gallery of the author's creations. We have
here the portraiture of one among that godless but

soft-hearted race of veterans who have alternately
bullied and blustered, or cried and whimpered, throughout many ages of fiction and melodrama. And in
depicting this type of character writers have invariably
felt it their bounden duty to give full prominence to
this fateful gift of swearing. With much discretion
the novelist has in the present instance invented a
subterfuge, which, while it does not rob Mr. Barley of
his idiosyncrasies of speech, leaves an amused and not
an offensive impression behind it. We are, in fact,
called in to assist at a very quiet piece of human con-
tradiction. We are presented to the prone Barley in
his state of helplessness and suffering, and at the same
time are given to understand that the sufferer derives
comfort and consolation from nothing so much as a
downright plunge into the torrent of bad language.

In these wandering musings of the complaining old
sea-captain there is suggested one of the many spells
that are exercised by the force of imprecation. There
is no paucity of men, whether dejected, dissatisfied or
penurious, who are wont to apostrophise some imagined
effigy of themselves, or to construct some idealised fabric
as a monument of their lives, and stalk it abroad for
their own and for other men's wonderment. And the
means they employ to spirit up these creations are not

dissimilar to those in use by Mr. Barley. By declaiming loudly against the ravages of a hard fate that lays them on their backs "like an old dead flounder," the mind is assisted to form a notion of the victims in their prime. By deploring the hardships of fallen fortune the eye of the sympathiser is carried instinctively back to bygone days of supposititious enjoyment. Imprecation is seldom absent from these incursions, being, in fact, urgently needed to do duty for closer argumentation. Again, as there are men so genial that they swear as a challenge to discontent, so there are men so discontented that they swear as a challenge to geniality.

This more unsociable aspect of the subject brings us perforce to the consideration of a term of swearing that contains no element of geniality. Of itself it can be accounted nothing but a mere outcome of bombast and vulgarity, appealing as it does to no known passion of the human mind. And yet so widespread is its influence, and so powerful its dominion, that it has been rung out and has reverberated probably more than any other in the great " fisc and exchequer " of abuse.

The expletive that it now behoves us to consider is one which has never been adequately treated in a book. We cannot disguise to ourselves that there is much in its unfortunate associations to render its occurrence still exceedingly painful. Originating in a senseless freak of language, it has by dint of circumstances become so noisome and offensive, that were it not for the undue power and influence it has usurped, we should hardly be disposed to treat of it at all. But when we mention that it is the ungainly adjective " bloody " that will occupy our attention for the next few pages, we must be allowed to add that it is with the view of stripping the term of its infamous significance, and if possible of dispelling from it the cloud of ill favour and of ill fame, that we venture with less reluctance to grapple with it.

With the full knowledge of the abhorrence it has imparted in our day, it is difficult to imagine any unsullied spring-time in the history of so sordid a word. It is the single particle of objuration that has not dared assume, as others have so frequently done, a jaunty or a rollicking demeanour. Not in the wildest days of Eastcheap revelry did it resound in any one key of vinous harmony. While other epithets may from time to time have received the sanction of conviviality, here is a word that is nothing unless discordant and acrimonious. It is the apt accompaniment of a whining tongue, the fit complement of a verjuice countenance.

Dirty drunkards hiccup it as they wallow on ale-house
floors.   Morose porters bandy it about on quays and
landing-stages.   From the low-lying quarters of the
towns the word buzzes in your ear with the confusion
of a Babel.   In the cramped narrow streets you are
deafened by its whirr and din, as it rises from the throats
of the chaffering multitude, from besotted men defiant
and vain-glorious in their drink, from shrewish women
hissing out rancour and menace in their harsh queru-
lous talk.

And yet to look back no further than to the youth
of Shakespeare, the word had no application beyond
such as was seemly, and its history was simple and
spotless and without reproach.   The one play of
'Macbeth' contains an unusual number of instances
of its occurrence, all written without any suspicion
of an *équivoque* and dwelt upon with an undoubting
sincerity that has become barely possible in a modern
work.   Indeed into such ill company has fallen this
true-minded adjective, that it is no longer competent
to be admitted to its proper place in an ordinary
publication.   Now and again strong protest has been
made against the hard sentence passed upon so well-
meaning a term, and authors of taste have demanded
its restitution to its former intellectual companionship.

In one of her " Letters to the Author of Orion," Mrs. E. B. Browning throws reserve upon the subject altogether to the winds, and insists upon embracing and cherishing this ill-starred word as a long lost acquaintance. But when Shakespeare wrote of

" The bloody house of life,"

there was no need for hesitation in shaping it. It was as unsullied and as transparent as any that might have been placed upon Imogen's lips or thrown by Hamlet into Ophelia's lap.

To account for the moral kidnapping that the word has undergone, it behoves us, strangely enough, to set face towards the Netherlands, and to hark back there to the campaigns of Flushing and Deventer, where Ben Jonson and others of his countrymen are shouldering their pikes under the generalship of Vere and Stanley. We shall then find it to have been one of the doubtful advantages that were gained by long years of Low Country soldiering. With the winds and tides that brought home the shoals of broken veterans, there was wafted to this country the flavour of foreign oaths, and among them the renown in speech of the German " blutig." Now " blutig " happened to be an inconsequent sort of particle that was employed in all the

N

dialects of Germany to denote a sense of the emphatic. It had been chosen throughout the German fatherland to minister to the wants of those defective degrees of comparison which are usually, however, found to be more or less admirably fitted to their purpose. It thus constituted itself a fourth degree, or extra-ultra-superlative. Like all verbal contrivances of this kind, it was more especially favoured among the less cultivated students of the forms of grammar, and seems at last to have become recognised as a convenient make-weight with which a reprobate soldiery were accustomed to balance their assertions.

It will be at once seen that this alien growth was capable of being readily transplanted to our soil in the shape of its literal counterpart. The circumstance of the words being so nearly identical is sufficient to account for the work of transposition being swiftly and effectually done. But beyond the mere accident of the respective tongues offering an exact literal equivalent, there was nothing in common between the German ."blutig" and the English correlative term. As evidenced by the purity of its antecedents, the latter derives nothing of the opprobrium that has devolved upon it by reason of any hereditary defects, far less on account of any of its inherent properties.

If Ben Jonson, who must have been brought face to face with this treasure in its natural home, does not seek to commend it to the keeping of his audiences, we may be sure that in his time at least it had attained no perceptible degree of literary currency. The comic dramatists were agreed at this period as to one canon of dramatic representation. They were accustomed to interlace the serious business of the comedy with mirth-moving interludes in which the more farcical characters of the piece were met together for the purpose, as it seemed, of besprinkling one another with the most aggravating and unpardonable abuse. The ingenuity of writers was ransacked to furnish material for this spirited by-play. Collections of all nationalities, and the reserves of all professions and handicrafts, were studiously drawn upon to furnish subject-matter for these wordy encounters. So far as they could help themselves, these shameless dramatists left no word unsaid that could increase the strife of tongues and raise a smile at the energy or possibly the grossness of the jargon. But as yet the epithet in question found no place in the prompt-book, and continued to be omitted from their vocabularies. Had Bohemian society even partially adopted it, it would be difficult to imagine the humours of the Artillery Garden, or the disorders of Ruffians'

N 2

Hall and Turnbull Street,* being glibly depicted by these outspoken playwrights without recourse being had to the services of this unconscionable adjective.

Shakespeare, himself probably the greatest exponent of the arts of scurrility, is totally exempt from any blameworthy intention in applying the word in the manner he so frequently uses it. But as years wore on the relish of foreign and far-travelled terms grew upon the public taste with surprising rapidity. A novelty must be extremely popular to enable it to become vulgar, and must even be liked before it can be thoroughly hated. "Bloody" was no exception to the rule, and enjoyed a brief day of estimation and patronage. Men of refinement and high culture adopted it rather as an article of scholarly adornment. Dryden uses it in this way, as does Swift. Play-writers heralded it on the stage, bestowing upon it the passport of literary sanction. In Sir George Etheredge's comedy, 'The Man of Mode,' a play that was witnessed by society with unbounded approval, the final stage in the process of abduction is plainly indicated. Says one of the characters, referring to the importunities of a tipsy vagrant, "Give him half-a-crown!" to which the

---

* "This same starved justice hath done nothing but prate to me of the wildness of his youth, and the feats he hath done about Turnbull Street."—2 *Henry IV.*, ii. 3.

other replies, " Not without he will promise to be bloody drunk ! "

In this way it would seem that the ball was set rolling. How the game has continued to be played we are most of us aware.   It calls for no particular skill on the part of the players, neither does the sport appear to decline for want of appreciation.   That it was received at its first incoming with a kind of *éclat* is not so surprising as is the strange attachment that for upwards of two centuries has been manifested by some ranks of society towards this discreditable word.   Its first flush of. approval may have been due to a certain element of whimsicality.   This at least is a sensation frequently conveyed by the occurrence of any meaningless affec- tation.   But, however this may be, it certainly was not at the first outset the mere grovelling and un- mitigated blackguardism which it was very shortly to be.   Dean Swift, full of wit and penury, writing from his London lodging to Stella in her comfortable Irish home, breaks into frequent outbursts at the scan- tiness of his comforts.   One October, when removed to Windsor, he is particularly tried by the severity of the autumnal weather, but the terms in which, address- ing a well-bred woman, he expresses his discomfort are striking, as showing the strange vicissitudes that language may undergo. "It grows bloody cold," he writes—and one may well imagine the chilled extremities of the reverend Dean—"it grows bloody cold, and I have no waistcoat."

In support of the view that there is nothing in the inherent properties of the word, or even in the range and frequency of its use, to account for the degraded position it has occupied in modern times, we have only to inquire whether any similar treatment has been the fate of the equivalent word in the language of France. What do we find? The French *sanglant* has even a wider sphere of application, and in its legitimate sense is even a greater favourite than our own adjective, but no such evil days have overtaken it. It can be used literally, as in the case of *viande sanglante*, or metaphorically, as in *un sanglant affront* or the aphorism *la sanglante raillerie blesse et ne corrige pas*, but not at any time is it found to deviate from the paths of decency. Everything, we consider, favours the idea we have formed of our stately English word proceeding soberly and reputably upon its honest course only to become the victim of this species of subversive horse-play at the hands of professed word-corrupters. Appreciative of the objurgatory advantages of the German *blutig*, they were indifferent to any affront they might pass upon the English tongue. From that time forward the word was branded as infamous. The manly ring that of right belonged to it, as instanced in such widely different productions as 'Piers Ploughman,'* or the 'Philaster' of Beaumont and Fletcher,† was becoming no longer possible. In recent days people have sometimes tried to reconcile these opposite tendencies and to endow the word with some amount of literary grace. The best attempt we have noticed in this direction is in a decree of the Government of Paraguay, which in August 1869 instructed its resident in this country that the presence of Francisco Lopez on Paraguayan soil was "a bloody sarcasm to civilisation." The gentleman who penned this document may have been·influenced by the example of Montaigne ‡ who admitted that he was accustomed to swear "more by imitation than complexion."

We have given what we believe to be the rational explanation of this most unwarrantable abduction of

---

* Where it is used in the sense of pertaining to kinship—"They are my blody brethren, quod pieres, for God boughte us alle."—'Piers Plowman,' vi. 210.

† Where it is met with as a verb—"With my own hands, I'll bloody my own sword."

‡ 'Montaigne's Essays,' ed. Hazlitt, iii. 120.

the word from its ancient uses. The English language, whose handmaid it was, has never put in a claim to the return of its services, and the professors of that language continue to be scared when they meet with the vulgar changeling at the corner of the street. The principal reason for abhorrence is probably founded upon misapprehension. It is assumed that the expression bears the savour of irreligion. The old Catholic oath of " blood and wounds " has been advanced as the origin. So far from this theory being well founded, we rather find the whole brood of Catholic oaths to have been swept away by the besom of the Reformation long before this expletive had raised its head. Neither are we able to support the contention that it takes its rise in the archaic " woundy," which perished in the same fires. It is quite clear that in this instance there is a marked and deep interval between the outgoing of the old form of scurrility and the advent of the new.

Without being understood to array ourselves on the side of this baneful expression, we desire to acquit it at once of all suspicion of irreligion. The men who originated it had furthest from their minds any inroad upon Catholic fervour. It was simply an imported ware, smuggled over in a soldier's knapsack. It was left to linger for a time upon the lips of sutlers and tapsters, and became the plaything of sergeants and backswordsmen, the broken companions who had smelt powder in the German wars. It took will and way from the mere caprices of imitation, that sufficed in time to render it palatable to the wiser and more sober of men. From the time of Dean Swift downwards, it has mostly suffered from being lamentably unfashionable. Association, which can do so much to influence and so little to regulate our dislikes, has insisted in linking this expletive with the classes that are taken to be the more sordid and malignant.

It may certainly come into play now and again among those people who are not averse to perpetrating a joke at the expense of a little casual loss of refinement. On these few occasions indeed it would even appear to be tinctured with some slight leaven of good-nature. Thus, the sailor appellation of Admiral Gambier—"old bloody Politeful"—must not be inveighed against too hardly. Neither need we be too squeamish over a once famous (or infamous) *bon mot* that passed current in a fashionable club where a certain learned and witty serjeant was wont to repair for his nightly rubber. One evening, after meeting with a stranger at the card-table who held a remarkable number of trumps, he had impatiently inquired

who had been his antagonist. On being told that the
player was Sir So-and-So, Bart., the serjeant is
reported to have at once rejoined that "he might have
known the fellow to have been a baronet by his bloody
hand!"

But there is a deeper and more solemn aspect in all
this than any that we have suggested or advanced.
No statistics, could any be collected, no known or ima-
ginable facts, could be trusted to convey the faintest
notion of the large place that is occupied in public
morals by the presence of this solitary piece of imprecation. Those who have opportunities of judging, will
be bound to admit that they see in it the plaything
and fondling of whole sections of citizen society. In
innumerable households, in countless families, if we
may so designate those fetid accumulations of humanity
that we must here be understood to indicate, there is
not an hour of the day—not a moment of the day—in
which this virulent and acrid malediction does not send
out its empty challenge. How can this moral choke-
damp, with all its fatal incrustations, fail to eat away
the supports and very framework of the dwelling. It
is hard perhaps to pass so heavy a sentence upon seemingly so slight an offence, but we are forced to believe
that the very existence and presence of this evil, in its

more rampant and impudent state, is of itself conclusive upon the point of good or evil government, upon the question of the predominance of human charity or of the blackest intensity of malice.

Neither is it the least regrettable circumstance that, considered as a piece of mingled vileness and effrontery, the word has been, and for the matter of that is still likely to be, a most telling and signal success. Those who have followed the writer at all closely will have already noticed the irresistible impulse of succeeding generations to secure to themselves the strongest possible anathema with which to carry on all manner of petty hostilities. But until the expletive that is now passing under our consideration was fairly launched upon society, no great measure of success can be said to have crowned their endeavours. The swearing of the pre-Reformation era may be adjudged the nearest approach to maledictory perfection, but even that system, admirable as it may have been from the point of view of an accomplished Boanerges of the time, was at best but an unstable and fluctuating one, and depended for its efficiency upon the swearer's own powers of invocation. As a rule no two oaths were alike, and men gave you the idea of thinking before they swore. So various a code could hardly be expected to meet with general success, it being as impossible for an individual to invent a really new oath—a new "bloody," for example—as it is said to be impossible to invent a new proverb or a new rhyme for the nursery. Imitations can of course be easily contrived, but the genuine product only arises through the seemingly spontaneous consent of approving multitudes. It was precisely in this way that the present abomination was generated. Not proceeding from any one man's store of virulence, but resulting from a long process of evolution and development, it at last springs into sudden life, in obedience, it would almost seem, to a nation's clamours. But no sooner was it called into this sphere of activity, than it became, we repeat, a gigantic success. It is the crown and apex of all bad language, the coping-stone of all systems of verbal aggression and abuse. By consent, as it were, of the general conscience it is allowed to have surpassed in vileness and intensity anything of the kind that has been intense or vile. That this stream of pollution should continue to flow, uninterruptedly and with increasing volume, through its inky channel, is one of the gloomiest and grimmest of the minor features of our social life.

APPENDIX.

Page 73. *Feminine Oaths.*—Among the number of feminine expletives may be reckoned Ophelia's adjuration " by Gis." The derivation has been a source of trouble to the commentators, who profess to see in it a corruption of Saint Cecily, an abbreviation of Saint Gislen, or else, as is more probable, a phonetic form of the letters I.H.S. But whatever its derivation, the oath was commonly attributed to the female sex. Thus, in Preston's ' Cambyses,' 1561, it is so employed ; and again in the pre-Shakespearian play of ' King John ' the nuns swear by Gis, and the monks, by way of distinction, take their oaths by Saint Withold. In ' Gammer Gurton's Needle ' the oath is placed in the mouth of the old housewife.

Page 84. *Foreign Oaths.*—We learn from Miss Bunbury's ' Summer in Northern Europe,' that the most common form of swearing in Sweden is a contraction of " God preserve us," and that hardly a sentence can escape from the lips of the lower orders without being supplemented by this expression—" bevars," the lengthened form of which is " Gud bevarva oss." Another form of imprecation is " Kors " or

" Kors Jesu," the Cross of Jesus, which the same writer intimates is in great request among the educated orders in Sweden.

Page 85. *Pre-Reformation Swearing.*—The testimony of Elyot in ' The Boke named the Governour,' written in 1531, is very conclusive upon the question. He says : " In dayly communication the mater savoureth nat, except it be as it were seasoned with horrible othes. As by the holy blode of Christe, his woundes whiche for our redemption he paynefully suffred, his glorious harte, as it were numbles chopped in pieces. Children (whiche abborreth me to remembre) do play with the armes and bones of Christe, as they were chery stones. The soule of God, whiche is incomprehensible, and nat to be named of any creature without a wonderfull reverence and drede, is nat onely the othe of great gentilmen, but also so indiscretely abused, that they make it (as I mought saye) their gonnes, wherwith they thunder out thretenynges and terrible menacis, whan they be in their fury, though it be at the damnable playe of dyse. The masse, in which honour-able ceremony is lefte unto us the memoriall of Christes glorious passion, with his corporall presence in fourme of breade, the invocation of the thre divine persones in one deitie, with all the hole company of blessed spirites and soules elect, is made by custome so simple an othe that it is nowe all most neglected and little regarded of the nobilitie, and is onely used among husbandemen and artificers, onelas some taylour or barbour, as well in his othes as in the excesse of his apparayle, will counterfaite and be lyke a gentilman."—ii. 252, *ed. Croft.*

So also Roger Hutchinson in his 'Image of God,' 1550 :—" You swearers and blasphemers which use to swear by God's heart, arms, nails, bowels, legs, and hands, learn what these things signify, and leave your abominable oaths."

Page 93. *Oath by the Swan.*—It was also the custom during the middle ages to serve with great pomp a pheasant, or some other noble bird, on which the knights swore to visit the Holy Land. In 1453, Philip the Good, Duke of Burgundy, vowed, *sur le faisan*, to go to the deliverance of Constantinople. His example was followed by the barons and knights assembled, who, in the words of Gibbon, " swore to God, the Virgin, the ladies and the pheasant."

Page 107. *A swearing corps d'élite.*—So long ago as the reign of Henry VIII. the expression "to swear like a lord " had become proverbial :—" For they wyll say he that swereth depe, swereth like a lorde."—' *The Governour,*' *by Sir T. Elyot,* 1531, *ed. Croft,* i. 275.

That the habit was making headway in high places may also be inferred from a bequest in one of the wills preserved in Doctors' Commons, in which the testator bequeathed a legacy of twenty shillings on condition that the legatee should desist from swearing. The will is that of Sir David Owen, a natural son of Owen Tudor, and is dated 1535.

Page 121. *Sir David Lindsay.*—Some idea of the fecundity of the old poet in the matter of expletives is conveyed by the catalogue of oaths culled from the '.Satyre of the Three Estaitis' and added to Chalmers' edition of Lindsay, published in 1806. The list is as follows :—

> "Be Cokis passion.
> Be Godis passion.
> Be Cok's deir passion.
> Be Cok's tois.
> Be God's wounds.
> Be God's croce.
> Be God's mother.
> Be God's breid.
> Be God's gown.
> Be God himsell.
> Be greit God that all has wrocht.
> Be him that made the mone.
> Be the gude Lord.
> Be him that wore the crown of thorn.
> Be him that bare the cruel crown of thorn.
> Be him that herryit hell.
> Be him that Judas sauld.
> Be the rude.
> Be the Trinity ; Be the haly Trinity.
> Be the sacrament ; Be the haly sacrament.
> Be the messe.
> Be him that our Lord Jesus sauld.
> Be him that deir Jesus sauld.
> Be our Lady ; Be Sainct Mary ; Be sweit Sainct Mary ; Be Mary bricht.

" Be Alhallows.
  Be Sanct James.
  Be Sanct Michell.
  Be Sanct Ann.
  Be Sanct Bryde; Be Bryde's bell.
  Be Sanct Geill; Be sweit Sanct Geill.
  Be Sanct Blais.
  Be Sanct Blane.
  Be Sanct Clone; Be Sanct Clune.
  Be Sanct Allan.
  Be Sanct Fillane.
  Be Sanct Tan.
  Be Sanct Dyonis of France.
  Be Sanct Maverne.
  Be the gude lady that me bare.
  Be my saul.
  Be my thrift.
  Be my Christendom.
  Be this day."

Against this list we may place a similar catalogue of objurgations extracted from the old play of 'Gammer Gurton's Needle,' acted at Cambridge in 1566. This work, ascribed to John Still, Bishop of Bath and Wells, very plainly depicts the condition of rustic manners at the period at which it was written :—

" By the mass (occurs 22 times).
  Gog's bones (4 times).
  Gog's soul (9 times).
  By my father's soul (2 times).
  Gog's sacrament (2 times).

" By my troth.

By God.

By sun and moon.

Gog's heart (6 times).

By God's mother.

Gog's bread (8 times).

By'r Lady (2 times).

By the cross.

By our dear lady of Boulogne.

Saint Dunstan.

Saint Dominic.

The three kings of Cologne.

By God and the devil too.

By bread and salt (2 times).

By him that Judas sold.

Gog's cross (2 times).

By Gog's malt (2 times).

Gog's death.

Gog's blessed body.

By God's blest (2 times).

By Gis.

By Saint Benet.

By my truth.

By Cock's mother dear.

By Saint Mary.

Gog's wounds (2 times).

By Cock's bones.

By All Hallows.

By my fay.

By my father's skin.

By God's pity (2 times).

Gog's sides (2 times).

Page 169. *The deuce!*—A specimen from the English version of 'Havelok the Dane,' edited by Sir F. Madden from the manuscript in the Laudian Collection in the Bodleian Library, may be appended:—

> "'Deus!' quoth he, 'hwat may this mene!'
> He calde bothe arwe men, and kene
> Knithes, and serganz swithe sleie,
> Mo than an hundred."—l. 2114.

Madden also refers the exclamation, *dash you* or *dase you*, from the Anglo-Saxon imprecation *datheit* which had been caught up from the Norman *deshait*.

LONDON: PRINTED BY WILLIAM CLOWES AND SONS, LIMITED, STAMFORD STREET
AND CHARING CROSS.

PUBLICATIONS

OF

J. C. NIMMO AND BAIN,

14 KING WILLIAM STREET, STRAND, LONDON, W.C.

A Handbook of Gastronomy

(BRILLAT-SAVARIN's " Physiologie du Goût "),

New and Complete Translation, with 52 original Etchings
by A. LALAUZE.

Printed on China Paper.

8vo, half parchment, gilt top, 42s.

NOTE.—*A limited Edition only of this book is printed.*

Ready in October.

The Fables of La Fontaine.

A REVISED TRANSLATION FROM THE FRENCH.

With 24 original full-page Etchings and Portrait by A. DELIERRE.

Super royal 8vo, cloth, gilt top, 31s. 6d.

Ready in October.

14 King William Street, Strand, London, W.C.

Types from Spanish Story;

OR,

THE OLD MANNERS AND CUSTOMS OF CASTILE.

By JAMES MEW.

With 36 Proof Etchings on Japanese paper by R. DE LOS RIOS.

Super royal 8vo, elegant and *recherché* Binding after the 18th Century, 31s. 6d.

Ready in October.

The Fan.

By OCTAVE UZANNE.

ILLUSTRATIONS BY PAUL AVRIL.

Royal 8vo, cloth, gilt top, 31s. 6d.

NOTE.—*This is an English Edition of the unique ana artistic work " L'Eventail," and is uniform in style and illustrations with " The Sunshade, Muff, and Glove."*

Ready in October.

The Dramatic Works of Richard Brinsley Sheridan.

WITH AN INTRODUCTORY SKETCH OF THE LIFE AND GENIUS OF SHERIDAN,

By RICHARD GRANT WHITE.

Three Portraits have been etched for this Edition—after the Painting by Sir Joshua Reynolds, the Drawing by Corbould, and the Sketch originally published in the *Gentleman's Magazine.*

In 3 vols. post 8vo, cloth.

NOTE.—*Only a limited number of this Edition has been printed.*

Ready in October.

A HANDSOME LARGE PAPER EDITION OF

The Works of Wm. Hickling Prescott.

In 15 Volumes 8vo, cloth (not sold separately).

With 30 Portraits printed on India paper.

Athenæum.

"In point of style Prescott ranks with the ablest English historians, and paragraphs may be found in his volumes in which the grace and elegance of Addison are combined with Robertson's majestic cadence and Gibbon's brilliancy."

J. Lothrop Motley.

"Wherever the English language is spoken over the whole earth his name is perfectly familiar. We all of us know what his place was in America. But I can also say that in eight years (1851-59) passed abroad I never met a single educated person of whatever nation that was not acquainted with his fame, and hardly one who had not read his works. No living American name is so widely spread over the whole world."

NOTE.—*Only a limited number of this Edition is printed.*

First three vols. ready in October.

The History of England,

FROM THE FIRST INVASION BY THE ROMANS TO THE ACCESSION OF WILLIAM AND MARY IN 1688.

By JOHN LINGARD, D.D.

Copyright Edition, with Ten Etched Portraits. In Ten Vols. demy 8vo, cloth, £5, 5s.

This New Copyright Library Edition of "Lingard's History of England," besides containing all the latest notes and emendations of the Author, with Memoir, in enriched with Ten Portraits, newly etched by Damman, of the following personages, viz. :—Dr. Lingard, Edward I., Edward III., Cardinal Wolsey, Cardinal Pole, Elizabeth, James I., Cromwell, Charles II., James II.

NOTE.—*The Edition is limited in number, and intending purchasers would do well by ordering early from their respective Booksellers.*

---

14 King William Street, Strand, London, W.C.

The Times.

" No greater service can be rendered to literature than the republication, in a handsome and attractive form, of works which time and the continued approbation of the world have made classical. . . . This new library edition of Dr. Lingard's ' History of England,' which has just been published in ten volumes, is an excellent reproduction of a work which had latterly been becoming somewhat scarce, and of which a new edition seems to be really wanted. . . . The accuracy of Lingard's statements on many points of controversy, as well as the genial sobriety of his view, is now recognised."

The Tablet.

" It is with the greatest satisfaction that we welcome this new edition of Dr. Lingard's ' History of England.' It has long been a desideratum. . . . No general history of England has appeared which can at all supply the place of Lingard, whose painstaking industry and careful research have dispelled many a popular delusion, whose candour always carries his reader with him, and whose clear and even style is never fatiguing. The type and get up of these ten volumes leave nothing to be desired, and they are enriched with excellent portraits in etching."

The Spectator.

" We are glad to see that the demand for Dr. Lingard's *England* still continues. Few histories give the reader the same impression of exhaustive study. This new edition is excellently printed, and illustrated with ten portraits of the greatest personages in our history."

Dublin Review.

" It is pleasant to notice that the demand for Lingard continues to be such that publishers venture on a well got-up library edition like the one before us. More than sixty years have gone since the first volume of the first edition was published ; many equally pretentious histories have appeared during that space, and have more or less disappeared since, yet Lingard lives—is still a recognised and respected authority."

The Scotsman.

" There is no need, at this time of day, to say anything in vindication of the importance, as a standard work, of Dr. Lingard's ' History of England.' For half a century it has been recognised as a literary achievement of the highest merit, and a monument of the erudition and research of the author. . . . His book is of the highest value, and should find a place on the shelves of every library. Its intrinsic merits are very great. The style is lucid, pointed, and puts no strain upon the reader ; and the printer and publisher have neglected nothing that could make this—what it is likely long to remain—the standard edition of a work of great historical and literary value."

Imaginary Conversations.

By WALTER SAVAGE LANDOR.

In Five Vols. crown 8vo, cloth, 30s.

FIRST SERIES—CLASSICAL DIALOGUES, GREEK AND ROMAN.

SECOND SERIES—DIALOGUES OF SOVEREIGNS AND STATESMEN.

THIRD SERIES—DIALOGUES OF LITERARY MEN.

FOURTH SERIES—DIALOGUES OF FAMOUS WOMEN.

FIFTH SERIES—MISCELLANEOUS DIALOGUES.

NOTE.— *This New Edition is printed from the last Edition of his Works, revised and edited by John Forster, and is published by arrangement with the Proprietors of the Copyright of Walter Savage Landor's Works.*

The Athenæum.

" The appearance of this tasteful reprint would seem to indicate that the present generation is at last waking up to the fact that it has neglected a great writer, and if so it is well to begin with Landor's most adequate work. It is difficult to overpraise the ' Imaginary Conversations.' The eulogiums bestowed on the ' Conversations ' by Emerson will, it is to be hoped, lead many to buy this book."

Scotsman.

"An excellent service has been done to the reading public by presenting to it, in five compact volumes, these ' Conversations.' Admirably printed on good paper, the volumes are handy in shape, and indeed the edition is all that could be desired. When this has been said, it will be understood what a boon has been conferred on the reading public ; and it should enable many comparatively poor men to enrich their libraries with a work that will have an enduring interest."

Literary World.

" That the ' Imaginary Conversations ' of Walter Savage Landor are not better known is no doubt largely due to their inaccessibility to most readers, by reason of their cost. This new issue, while handsome enough to find a place in the best of libraries, is not beyond the reach of the ordinary bookbuyer."

Edinburgh Review.

" How rich in scholarship ! how correct, concise, and pure in style ! how full of imagination, wit, and humour ! how well informed, how bold in speculation, how various in interest, how universal in sympathy! In these dialogues—making allowance for every shortcoming or excess—the most familiar and the most august shapes of the past are reanimated with vigour, grace, and beauty. We are in the high and goodly company of wits and men of letters; of churchmen, lawyers, and statesmen; of party-men, soldiers, and kings; of the most tender, delicate, and noble women; aud of figures that seem this instant to have left for us the Agora or the Schools of Athens, the Forum or the Senate of Rome."

The Sunshade, Muff, and Glove.

By OCTAVE UZANNE.

ILLUSTRATIONS BY PAUL AVRIL.

Royal 8vo, cloth, gilt top, 31s. 6d.

NOTE.—*This is an English Edition of the unique and artistic work "L'Ombrelle," recently published in Paris, and now difficult to be procured. No new Edition in French to be produced.*

This Edition has been printed at the press of Monsieur QUANTIN with the same care and wonderful taste as was his French Edition.

Glasgow Herald.

" ' I have but collected a heap of foreign flowers, and brought of my own only the string which binds them together' is the fitting quotation with which M. Uzanne closes the preface to his volume on Woman's Ornaments. The monograph on the Sunshade, called by the author 'a little tumbled fantasy,' occupies fully one-half of the volume. It begins with a pleasant invented mythology of the parasol; glances at the sunshade in all countries and times; mentions many famous umbrellas; quotes a number of clever sayings. . . . To these remarks on the spirit of the book it is necessary to add that the body of it is a dainty marvel of paper, type, and binding; and that what meaning it has looks out on the reader through a hundred argus-eyes of many-tinted *photogravures*, exquisitely designed by M. Paul Avril."

Athenæum.

"The letterpress comprises much amusing 'chit-chat,' and is more solid than it pretends to be. The illustrations contain a good deal that is acceptable on account of their spirit and variety. . . . This *brochure* is worth reading, nay, we think it is worth keeping."

14 King William Street, Strand, London, W.C.

Scotsman.

"This book is to be prized, if only because of its text. But this is by no means its sole, we might say, its chief attraction. M. Uzanne has had the assistance of M. Paul Avril as illustrator, and that artist has prepared many designs of singular beauty and gracefulness. It would be difficult to speak too highly of them ; they have a piquancy and grace which is in the highest degree attractive. It is one of the prettiest and most attractive volumes we have seen for many a day."

The Complete Angler;

OR,

THE CONTEMPLATIVE MAN'S RECREATION,

Of IZAAK WALTON and CHARLES COTTON.

Edited by JOHN MAJOR.

A New Edition, with 8 original Etchings (2 Portraits and 6 Vignettes), two impressions of each, one on Japanese and one on Whatman paper ; also, 74 Engravings on Wood, printed on China Paper throughout the text.

8vo, cloth, gilt top, 31s. 6d.

The Times.

"Messrs. Nimmo & Bain, who seem resolved to take a leading place in the production of attractive volumes, have now issued a beautiful edition of Walton & Cotton's 'Angler.' The paper and printing leave nothing to be desired, and the binding is very tasteful."

The Field.

"As works of art Mr. Tourrier's etchings are admirable, and the printers and publishers have done their work admirably. . . A very handsome book, and one which will form a satisfactory present to many an angler."

Daily Telegraph.

"To the grand numerical monuments of this book's universal popularity is now added a sumptuous reprint of the 1844 edition, with eight brilliant etchings. The woodcuts, fresh and beautiful, are gems of an art now endangered by modern requirements of haste. This volume, so carefully reprinted, is a choice and welcome addition to the piscatorial library."

⚛ld Spanish Romances.

Illustrated with Etchings.

In 12 Vols. crown 8vo, parchment boards or cloth, 7s. 6d. per vol.

THE HISTORY of DON QUIXOTE DE LA MANCHA.
Translated from the Spanish of MIGUEL DE CERVANTES
SAAVEDRA by MOTTEUX. With copious Notes (including the
Spanish Ballads), and an Essay on the Life and Writings of
CERVANTES by JOHN G. LOCKHART. Preceded by a Short
Notice of the Life and Works of PETER ANTHONY MOTTEUX
by HENRI VAN LAUN. Illustrated with Sixteen Original
Etchings by R. DE LOS RIOS. Four Volumes.

LAZARILLO DE TORMES. By Don DIEGO MENDOZA.
Translated by THOMAS ROSCOE. And **GUZMAN D'ALFA-
RACHE.** By MATEO ALEMAN. Translated by BRADY.
Illustrated with Eight Original Etchings by R. DE LOS RIOS.
Two Volumes.

ASMODEUS. By LE SAGE. Translated from the French.
Illustrated with Four Original Etchings by R. DE LOS RIOS.

THE BACHELOR OF SALAMANCA. By LE SAGE.
Translated from the French by JAMES TOWNSEND. Illustrated
with Four Original Etchings by R. DE LOS RIOS.

VANILLO GONZALES; or, The Merry Bachelor. By LE
SAGE. Translated from the French. Illustrated with Four
Original Etchings by R. DE LOS RIOS.

THE ADVENTURES OF GIL BLAS OF SANTIL-
LANE. Translated from the French of LE SAGE by TOBIAS
SMOLLETT. With Biographical and Critical Notice of LE
SAGE by GEORGE SAINTSBURY. New Edition, carefully
revised. Illustrated with Twelve Original Etchings by R. DE
LOS RIOS. Three Volumes.

NOTE.—*A small number of above was printed on Medium 8vo
Laid Paper.*

14 King William Street, Strand, London, W.C.

The Times.

"This prettily printed and prettily illustrated collection of Spanish Romances deserve their welcome from all students of seventeenth century literature."

Daily Telegraph.

"A handy and beautiful edition of the works of the Spanish masters of romance. . . . We may say of this edition of the immortal work of Cervantes that it is most tastefully and admirably executed, and that it is embellished with a series of striking etchings from the pen of the Spanish artist De los Rios."

Scotsman.

"Handy in form, they are well printed from clear type, and are got up with much elegance; the etchings are full of humour and force. The reading public have reason to congratulate themselves that so neat, compact, and well arranged an edition of romances that can never die is put within their reach. The publishers have spared no pains with them."

Saturday Review.

"Messrs. Nimmo & Bain have just brought out a series of Spanish prose works in twelve finely got-up volumes."

Old English Romances.

Illustrated with Etchings.

In 12 Vols. crown 8vo, parchment boards or cloth, 7s. 6d. per vol.

THE LIFE AND OPINIONS OF TRISTRAM SHANDY, GENTLEMAN. By LAURENCE STERNE. In Two Vols. With Eight Etchings by DAMMAN from Original Drawings by HARRY FURNISS.

THE OLD ENGLISH BARON: A GOTHIC STORY. By CLARA REEVE.

ALSO

THE CASTLE OF OTRANTO: A GOTHIC STORY. By HORACE WALPOLE. In One Vol. With Two Portraits and Four Original Drawings by A. H. TOURRIER, Etched by DAMMAN.

THE ARABIAN NIGHTS ENTERTAINMENTS. In Four Vols. Carefully Revised and Corrected from the Arabic by JONATHAN SCOTT, I.L.D., Oxford. With Nineteen Original Etchings by AD. LALAUZE.

THE HISTORY OF THE CALIPH VATHEK. By
WM. BECKFORD. With Notes, Critical and Explanatory.

ALSO

RASSELAS, PRINCE OF ABYSSINIA. By SAMUEL
JOHNSON. In One Vol. With Portrait of BECKFORD, and
Four Original Etchings, designed by A. H. TOURRIER, and
Etched by DAMMAN.

ROBINSON CRUSOE. By DANIEL DEFOE. In Two Vols.
With Biographical Memoir, Illustrative Notes, and Eight
Etchings by M. MOUILLERON, and Portrait by L. FLAMENG.

GULLIVER'S TRAVELS. By JONATHAN SWIFT. With
Five Etchings and Portrait by AD. LALAUZE.

A SENTIMENTAL JOURNEY. By LAURENCE STERNE.

ALSO

A TALE OF A TUB. By JONATHAN SWIFT. In One Vol.
With Five Etchings and Portrait by ED. HEDOUIN.

NOTE.—*A small number of above was printed on Medium 8vo
Laid Paper.*

The Times.

"Among the numerous handsome reprints which the publishers of
the day vie with each other in producing, we have seen nothing of
greater merit than this series of twelve volumes. Those who have read
these masterpieces of the last century in the homely garb of the old
editions may be gratified with the opportunity of perusing them with
the advantages of large clear print and illustrations of a quality which
is rarely bestowed on such re-issues. The series deserves every com-
mendation."

Athenæum.

"A well-printed and tasteful issue of the 'Thousand and One
Nights.' The volumes are convenient in size, and illustrated with
Lalauze's well-known etchings."

Magazine of Art.

"The text of the new four-volume edition of the 'Thousand and
One Nights' just issued by Messrs. Nimmo & Bain is that revised by
Jonathan Scott, from the French of Galland; it presents the essentials
of these wonderful stories with irresistible authority and directness, and,
as mere reading, it is as satisfactory as ever. The edition, which is
limited to a thousand copies, is beautifully printed and remarkably well

produced. It is illustrated with twenty etchings by Lalauze. . . . In another volume of this series Beckford's wild and gloomy 'Vathek' appears side by side with Johnson's admirable 'Rasselas.'"

Glasgow Herald.

"The merits of this new issue lie in exquisite clearness of type, completeness; notes and biographical notices, short and pithy; and a number of very fine etchings and portraits. In the 'Robinson Crusoe,' besides the well-known portrait of Defoe by Flameng, there are eight exceedingly beautiful etchings by Mouilleron. . . . In fine keeping with the other volumes of the series, uniform in style and illustrations, and as one of the volumes of their famous Old English Romances, Messrs. Nimmo & Bain have also issued the 'Rasselas' of Johnson and the 'Vathek' of Beckford."

Westminster Review.

"Messrs. Nimmo & Bain have added to their excellent series of 'Old English Romances' three new volumes, of which two are devoted to 'Tristram Shandy,' while the third contains 'The Old English Baron' and 'The Castle of Otranto.' Take them as they stand, and without attributing to them any qualities but what they really possess, the whole series was well worth reprinting in the elegant and attractive form in which they are now presented to us."

The Imitation of Christ.

FOUR BOOKS.

Translated from the Latin by Rev. W. BENHAM, B.D.,

Rector of St. Edmund, King and Martyr, Lombard Street.

With ten Illustrations by J. P. LAURENS, etched by LEOPOLD FLAMENG.

Crown 8vo, cloth or parchment boards, 10s. 6d.

Scotsman.

"We have not seen a more beautiful edition of 'The Imitation of Christ' than this one for many a day."

Magazine of Art.

"This new edition of the 'Imitation' may fairly be regarded as a work of art. It is well and clearly printed; the paper is excellent; each page has its peculiar border, and it is illustrated with ten etchings. Further than that the translation is Mr. Benham's we need say nothing more."

Essays from the "North American Review."

Edited by ALLEN THORNDIKE RICE.

Demy 8vo, cloth, 7s. 6d.

Saturday Review.

"A collection of interesting essays from the *North American Review*, beginning with a criticism on the works of Walter Scott, and ending with papers written by Mr. Lowell and Mr. O. W. Holmes. The variety of the essays is noteworthy."

Alain René Le Sage. (1668-1747.)

A SHORT HISTORY OF THE

LIFE AND WRITINGS OF ALAIN RENÉ LE SAGE,

The Author of "Gil Blas,"

Who was born at Sarzean on the 8th of May 1668, and died at Boulogne on the 17th November 1747.

By GEORGE SAINTSBURY.

Medium 8vo, 50 pp., paper covers, 3s. 6d.

Peter Anthony Motteux. (1660-1718.)

A SHORT HISTORY OF THE LATE

MR. PETER ANTHONY MOTTEUX,

A Native of France,

Whilom Dramatist, China Merchant, and Auctioneer,

Who departed this life on the 18th of February 1718 (old style), being then precisely 58 years old.

By HENRI VAN LAUN.

Medium 8vo, 43 pp., paper covers, 3s. 6d.

The American Patent Portable Book-Case.

For Students, Barristers, Home Libraries, &c.

THIS Book-case will be found to be made of very solid and durable material, and of a neat and elegant design. The shelves may be adjusted for books of any size, and will hold from 150 to 300 volumes. As it requires neither nails, screws, or glue, it may be taken to pieces in a few minutes, and reset up in another room or house, where it would be inconvenient to carry a large frame.

Full Height, 5 ft. 11½ in.; Width, 3 ft. 8 in.; Depth of Shelf, 10½ in.

Black Walnut, price £6, 6s. nett.

"The accompanying sketch illustrates a handy portable book-case of American manufacture, which Messrs. NIMMO & BAIN have provided. It is quite different from an ordinary article of furniture, such as upholsterers inflict upon the public,

14 King William Street, Strand, London, W.C.

as it is designed expressly for holding the largest possible number of books in the smallest possible amount of space. One of the chief advantages which these book-cases possess is the ease with which they may be taken apart and put together again. No nails or metal screws are employed, nothing but the hand is required to dismantle or reconstruct the case. The parts fit together with mathematical precision; and, from a package of boards of very moderate dimensions, a firm and substantial book-case can be erected in the space of a few minutes. Appearances have by no means been overlooked; the panelled sides, bevelled edges, and other simple ornaments, give to the cases a very neat and tasteful look. For students, or others whose occupation may involve frequent change of residence, these book-cases will be found most handy and desirable, while, at the same time, they are so substantial, well-made, and convenient, that they will be found equally suitable for the library at home."

Select List from the Catalogue of J. & A. Churchill,

PUBLISHERS, NEW BURLINGTON STREET,

As supplied by J. C. NIMMO & BAIN.

Catalogue of the Publications of W. H. Allen & Co.,

PUBLISHERS, WATERLOO PLACE,

As supplied by J. C. NIMMO & BAIN.

BOOK-CORNER PROTECTORS.

Metal Tips carefully prepared for placing on the Corners of Books to preserve them from injury while passing through the Post Office or being sent by Carrier.

Extract from "The Times," April 18th.

"That the publishers and booksellers of America second the efforts of the Post Office authorities in endeavouring to convey books without damage happening to them is evident from the tips which they use to protect the corners from injury during transit."

1s. 6d. per Gross, nett.

J. C. NIMMO & BAIN,

14 KING WILLIAM STREET, STRAND, LONDON, W.C.